Messages from Space:

The Solar System and Beyond

Teacher's Guide

Grades 5–8

Skills
Observing, Inferring, Drawing Conclusions, Designing and Making Models, Visualizing, Explaining, Communicating, Decoding Binary Messages

Concepts
Astronomy, Solar System, Planetary System, Origin of Planetary Systems, Star Lifezones, Search for Extraterrestrial Intelligence (SETI), Relative Sizes and Distances of Solar and Other Star System Bodies

Themes
Models and Simulations, Systems and Interactions, Patterns of Change, Scale, Stability, Evolution, Diversity and Unity

Mathematics Strands
Number, Measurement, Pattern, Logic and Language, Statistics and Probability

Nature of Science and Mathematics
Science and Technology, Creativity and Constraints, Interdisciplinary, Real-Life Applications

by

Kevin Beals, John Erickson, and **Cary Sneider**

LHS GEMS

Great Explorations in Math and Science
Lawrence Hall of Science
University of California at Berkeley

Cover Design
Kyle C. Jennison, Dublin, Ohio, and Charlie Hall, Eureka, Missouri
Student Art Contest Winners! (adapted by Rose Craig and Carol Bevilacqua)

Design and Illustrations
Lisa Klofkorn

Photographs
Richard Hoyt
Laurence Bradley
Cary Sneider

Lawrence Hall of Science, University of California,
Berkeley, CA 94720-5200

Director: Ian Carmichael

Publication of *Messages from Space* was made possible by a grant from the Employees Community Fund of Boeing California and the Boeing Corporation (originally from the McDonnell Douglas Foundation and Employees Community Fund). The GEMS Program and the Lawrence Hall of Science greatly appreciate this support.

Initial support for the origination and publication of the GEMS series was provided by the A.W. Mellon Foundation and the Carnegie Corporation of New York. Under a grant from the National Science Foundation, GEMS Leader's Workshops have been held across the country. GEMS has also received support from: the McDonnell-Douglas Foundation and the McDonnell-Douglas Employee's Community Fund; Employees Community Fund of Boeing California and the Boeing Corporation; the Hewlett Packard Company; the people at Chevron USA; the William K. Holt Foundation; Join Hands, the Health and Safety Educational Alliance; the Microscopy Society of America (MSA); the Shell Oil Company Foundation; and the Crail-Johnson Foundation. GEMS also gratefully acknowledges the contribution of word processing equipment from Apple Computer, Inc. This support does not imply responsibility for statements or views expressed in publications of the GEMS program. For further information on GEMS leadership opportunities, or to receive a catalog and the *GEMS Network News*, please contact GEMS at the address and phone number below. We also welcome letters to the *GEMS Network News*.

Printed on recycled paper with soy-based inks.

International Standard Book Number: 0-924886-17-X

COMMENTS WELCOME !

Great Explorations in Math and Science (GEMS) is an ongoing curriculum development project. GEMS guides are revised periodically, to incorporate teacher comments and new approaches. We welcome your criticisms, suggestions, helpful hints, and any anecdotes about your experience presenting GEMS activities. Your suggestions will be reviewed each time a GEMS guide is revised. Please send your comments to: GEMS Revisions, c/o Lawrence Hall of Science, University of California, Berkeley, CA 94720-5200. The phone number is (510) 642-7771 and the fax number is (510) 643-0309. You can also reach us by e-mail at gems@uclink4.berkeley.edu or visit our web site at **www.lhs.berkeley.edu/GEMS**.

Great Explorations in Math and Science (GEMS) Program

The Lawrence Hall of Science (LHS) is a public science center on the University of California at Berkeley campus. LHS offers a full program of activities for the public, including workshops and classes, exhibits, films, lectures, and special events. LHS is also a center for teacher education and curriculum research and development.

Over the years, LHS staff have developed a multitude of activities, assembly programs, classes, and interactive exhibits. These programs have proven to be successful at the Hall and should be useful to schools, other science centers, museums, and community groups. A number of these guided-discovery activities have been published under the Great Explorations in Math and Science (GEMS) title, after an extensive refinement and adaptation process that includes classroom testing of trial versions, modifications to ensure the use of easy-to-obtain materials, with carefully written and edited step-by-step instructions and background information to allow presentation by teachers without special background in mathematics or science.

Staff

Director: Jacqueline Barber
Associate Director: Kimi Hosoume
Associate Director/Principal Editor: Lincoln Bergman
Mathematics Curriculum Specialist: Jaine Kopp
GEMS Network Director: Carolyn Willard
GEMS Workshop Coordinator: Laura Tucker
Staff Development Specialists: Lynn Barakos, Katharine Barrett, Kevin Beals, Ellen Blinderman, Gigi Dornfest, John Erickson, Stan Fukunaga, Philip Gonsalves, Linda Lipner, Karen Ostlund, Debra Sutter
Financial Assistant: Alice Olivier
Distribution Coordinator: Karen Milligan
Workshop Administrator: Terry Cort

Materials Manager: Vivian Tong
Distribution Representative: Felicia Roston
Shipping Assistant: Jodi Harskamp
Director of Marketing and Promotion: Matthew Osborn
Senior Editor: Carl Babcock
Editor: Florence Stone
Principal Publications Coordinator: Kay Fairwell
Art Director: Lisa Haderlie Baker
Senior Artists: Carol Bevilacqua, Rose Craig, Lisa Klofkorn
Staff Assistants: Trina Huynh, Jennifer Lee, Jacqueline Moses, Chastity Pérez, Dorian Traube

Contributing Authors

Jacqueline Barber
Katharine Barrett
Kevin Beals
Lincoln Bergman
Ellen Blinderman
Susan Brady
Beverly Braxton

Kevin Cuff
Linda De Lucchi
Gigi Dornfest
Jean Echols
John Erickson
Philip Gonsalves
Jan M. Goodman

Alan Gould
Catherine Halversen
Kimi Hosoume
Susan Jagoda
Jaine Kopp
Linda Lipner
Larry Malone

Cary I. Sneider
Craig Strang
Debra Sutter
Herbert Thier
Jennifer Meux White
Carolyn Willard

Reviewers

We would like to thank the following educators who reviewed, tested, or coordinated the reviewing of *Messages from Space* and *Math on the Menu*. Their critical comments and recommendations, based on classroom and schoolwide presentation of these activities nationwide, contributed significantly to this GEMS publication. Their participation in this review process does not necessarily imply endorsement of the GEMS program or responsibility for statements or views expressed. Their role is an invaluable one; feedback is carefully recorded and integrated as appropriate into the publications. **THANK YOU!**

ARIZONA

Kyrene de Las Manitas Elementary, Tempe
Jeanne Anciaux
Lori Conroy
*Alice Maro
Pam Parzych

ARKANSAS

Fox Meadow Elementary School, Jonesboro
Sharon Hill
Kay Martin
*Dr. Ruby Midkiff
Linda Simpson

CALIFORNIA

Washington School, Alameda
*Traci Alligrati

Marin Elementary, Albany
Kenneth Fujita
Marlene Keret
Diane Meltzer
*Sonia Zulpo

Antioch Middle School, Antioch
Leslie Adams
*Mark Balken
Joe Smyle
Lynette Wall

Creekside Middle School, Castro Valley
*Mary Cummins Bird
Victoria Mah
Scott Malfatti
Nancy Wilder

Windrush School, El Cerrito
*Joanne Chace
Nicola Furman
JoAnne Rubio
Martha Vlahos

Emery Middle School, Emeryville
Steve Hambright
Mark Sneed
*Letecia Trotter-Brock

Stanley Intermediate School, Lafayette
*Mike Meneghetti
Dixie Mohan
Jan Winter

Joaquin Miller Elementary, Oakland
Karen DeCotis
Jan Matsuoka
*Joyce Melton

Manzanita School, Oakland
Geraldine Ferry
Anna Gorman
*Ashley Keller
Hattie Saunders
Felicia Sexsmith

Markham School, Oakland
*Sharon Kerr
Lynn Martin
Margaret Wright

St. Elizabeths Elementary School, Oakland
*Christine Bertko
Jim Chaky

Ellerhorst Elementary School, Pinole
*Jody Anderson
Nancy Cabral
Trudy Jensen
Kathy Paulson
Nancy Richtik

Seaview Elementary, San Pablo
Charise Calone
Patti Fabian
Krista Hansler
Christi Silveira
*Barbara Taylor

COLORADO

Kunsmiller Middle School, Denver
*Juan Carlos Galván
Sandra V. Jaime
George Pullis
Patsy Trujillo

Thank You!

MICHIGAN

John Page Middle School, Madison Heights
Barb Buezynski
Kay Davis
Jackie Jones
*Mike Mansour
Ralph Shepard

MISSOURI

Mullanphy Botanical Garden Investigative Learning Center, St Louis
**Barbara Addelson
*Diane Dymond
Martha Eckhoff
Katherine Leslie
Effie Miller
Dawn Tofari

NEVADA

Our Lady of the Snows Parochial School, Reno
Ann Boeser
*Dave Brancamp
Teresa Kennedy
Vilia Natchez

NEW HAMPSHIRE

Milford Elementary School, Milford
Heidi Blake
Jennifer Maurais
*Carol McKinney
Kathy Parker

TENNESSEE

Cosby High School, Cosby
Steve Sharp

University of Tennessee-Appalachian Rural System Initiative, Knoxville
**Terry Lashley

Centerview Elementary School, Newport
Kathy Holt

Cocke County High School, Newport
*Missy Biddle
Sheila Huskey

Parrottsville Elementary School, Newport
Randy Winter

TEXAS

Birdville ISD, Haltom City
**Gail Knight

Haltom High School, Haltom City
Cindy Hostings

Haltom Middle School, Haltom City
Liane Lovett

North Ridge Middle School, North Richland Hills
Jennifer Ford

Murray Fly Elementary School, Odessa
Alice Derras
Sandra McAdams
*Kym Monacelli

Richland Middle School, Richland Hills
Shannon Reeves

WASHINGTON

Hearthwood Elementary, Vancouver
Kirsten Comish
*Susan Crawford
Sara Myers
Linda Roland

WEST VIRGINIA

Spencer Middle School, Spencer
*William E. Chapman Jr.
Shelba Fountaine
Barbara J. Keen
David Ruediger

* On-Site Coordinator
** Regional Coordinator

"Messages from Space"

Acknowledgments

The trial test teachers and their students who took part in the testing process are listed at the front of this guide. Their comments and criticisms greatly aided in the improvement of this unit. We are particularly appreciative of the large amounts of student work teachers sent us, a small portion of which we've adapted for inclusion in the guide. We also thank and heartily congratulate Kyle C. Jennison of Dublin, Ohio, and Charlie Hall of Eureka, Missouri, the student winners of the GEMS art cover contest, whose original works were adapted by GEMS designers for the front and back covers.

The activity that features the fictional message from outer space (Activity 1) was originated by Cary Sneider, former GEMS Science Curriculum Specialist, and previously copyrighted by The Regents of the University of California. Like many GEMS activities, it was devised for classes offered at the Lawrence Hall of Science in the 1980s. Cary also played a major role in conceptualizing this guide, with Kevin Beals and John Erickson, as they selected this sequence from many activities, originated new ones, and revised the unit as a GEMS guide. Thanks as well to Alan Gould and the Planetarium Activities for Student Success (PASS) series (see page 142) from which several activities and illustrations were adapted.

This guide also grew out of a curriculum development project, *Life in the Universe,* led by the SETI Institute in Mountain View, California, in collaboration with the Lawrence Hall of Science (LHS), and funded by the National Science Foundation, (NSF MDR-9150120) and the National Aeronautics and Space Administration (NASA Cooperative Agreement NCC-2-336). The resulting *Life in the Universe* (LITU) series is an outstanding educational resource for teachers and students in grades 3–9. These extensive teacher's guides include one for grades 3–4, three for grades 5–6, and two for middle school, grades 7–9. One of the guides for grades 5–6 is entitled *Evolution of a Planetary System,* and several of the activities in this GEMS guide are similar to those in *Evolution of a Planetary System.* In connection with Activity 2 in this GEMS guide, "Somewhere in the Milky Way—Star Types and Lifezones," we acknowledge two "missions" or lessons from the LITU *Evolution of a Planetary System:* "Mission 4: Types of Stars: Is Our Sun Unique?" and "Mission 5: Lifezones of Stars: Not Too Hot, Not Too Cold, But Just Right." Relating to two sessions in Activity 3 in this GEMS guide, "Our Neighborhood in the Milky Way—The Solar System," we likewise acknowledge "Mission 3: Formation of Planetary Systems: Do All Stars Have Planets?" in the LITU guide. For Activity 5 in this GEMS guide, "Making a Planetary System," we acknowledge "Mission 6: Building a

Model Planetary System: Creating Your Own 'Solar' System" from the LITU guide. For more information on the *Life in the Universe* series, see the "Resources" section on page 141, or visit the SETI Institute web site at http://www.seti.org to preview the LITU teacher's guides and download sample lessons.

The development of the LITU series involved many talented scientists and educators from both the SETI Institute and the Lawrence Hall of Science (including two of this guide's authors) as well as teachers in San Francisco Bay Area schools. The Principal Investigator for the LITU series was Dr. Jill Tarter at the SETI Institute; she currently heads the SETI search as the Bernard M. Oliver Chair for SETI. The authors for *The Evolution of a Planetary System* were Dr. Jill Tarter, Cara Stoneburner, Victoria Johnson, Dr. Seth Shostak, and Emily Theobald (SETI Institute); Kevin Beals, Lisa Dettloff, Alan Gould, John Hewitt, Dr. Cary Sneider, and Lisa Walenceus (Lawrence Hall of Science); Mary-Chafe-Powles, Woodside Elementary School, Concord, California; Betty Merritt, Longfellow Intermediate School, Berkeley, California; and Dr. David Milne, Evergreen State College, Olympia, Washington.

It should be noted that although the activities detailed above share a common collaborative origin, their new presentation in *Messages from Space* reflects additional development, modification and adaptation by the authors and other GEMS staff, and revision in accordance with feedback from teachers during the GEMS trial-testing process.

We are particularly appreciative of the expert and thorough review of the national trial version of this guide by two SETI Institute representatives, Edna DeVore, Director of Educational Programs, and Dr. Seth Shostak, Public Programs Scientist, whose book *Sharing the Universe* is described in the "Resources" section. Their review included important global comments, many issues of scientific accuracy, and precise corrections, which greatly improved the quality of this guide. Edna also provided information and text on the SETI Institute, and Seth provided several photographs. Any continuing errors or issues of interpretation are of course the responsibility of the authors and the GEMS program.

Finally, we are most especially indebted to John Hewitt of the Lawrence Hall of Science for his careful and intensive review of much of the specific astronomical information in this guide—especially the fact sheets on the planets, moons, and solar system—and the many issues of size, scale, and distance. His concern for accuracy and attention to detail are truly worthy of astronomical praise!

Special Dedication

As this book entered final publication stages, we were deeply saddened to learn of the untimely death of John Hewitt, LHS instructor and indefatigable "sidewalk astronomer." John taught after school and summer camp classes and was one of the primary presenters of the Hall's interactive planetarium programs. His encyclopedic knowledge of astronomy and related educational resources contributed to Messages from Space *and to several other GEMS guides. (John also devised an experiment for the Hubble spacecraft, which concerned the possibility of inferring the existence of "Oort" comet clouds in other star systems!) In recognition of John's educational achievements and scientific commitment, this guide, with activities that encourage students and teachers to explore topics near and dear to his heart and intellect, is dedicated to him.*

Contents

"Do there exist many worlds, or is there but a single world? This is one of the most noble and exalted questions in the study of Nature."

Albertus Magnus, thirteenth century

Introduction

The public's fascination with lifeforms from outer space seems to be insatiable. We are surrounded by books, television shows, movies, and tabloids—and the flood shows no sign of subsiding. Most material on this subject is in the realm of fantasy and entertainment. This unit introduces students to possibilities that are even more exciting because they are real.

Messages from Space touches only very lightly on the popular unscientific notions of "aliens" from outer space and UFOs. It is not primarily a "debunking" curriculum. It focuses instead on some of the questions that scientists must tackle when they explore the possibilities of extraterrestrial intelligence. In doing so, this unit exposes students to the scientific view of our place in the cosmos, giving them the background to critically evaluate unscientific claims, such as the often sensationalized possibility of "alien" invasion.

In this respect, this unit seeks to convey two key things: first, that there is a strong chance of some form of life existing out there somewhere; and second, that the incredibly vast distances involved mean that the chances of any of these lifeforms actually coming to Earth are minuscule indeed!

Astronomy is an especially exciting science right now. With the new technologies now available, astronomers are making new discoveries left and right. Some phenomena that have until recently only been hypothesized are now showing up through analysis of images captured by ever more powerful telescopes.

Through the mass media, the public has an opportunity to watch science in action, as ideas evolve, are verified, disproved, or improved. Whether it be water on the Moon, the discovery of planets around distant stars, or recent evidence that indicates the Universe will keep expanding forever, human knowledge of the vast spaces around our tiny planet is growing "astronomically!"

Many curricula tap into students' natural fascination with space, particularly relating to the solar system. This guide does so too, but from a different angle. Instead of focusing on facts about each planet and the memorization of numbers and names, we've chosen to challenge students to use these facts to tackle some of the bigger questions about space and the solar system.

Please note that we have reproduced NASA images in color on a special back cover flap. Since these images are in the public domain, you could color copy some sets of these and cut them into cards for students to have as they start their work on solar system travel brochures in Activity 3, Session 2. Or you could use them in other ways. As many teachers know, NASA has many outstanding educational resources available. In the "Resources" section of this guide. there is contact information on the "NASA Teacher Resource Center Network"—look for the one near you. There are also a number of web sites listed in this guide, many of which are great sources for additional images of the solar system and beyond.

Note: Some of the photographs in this guide were taken during the testing of earlier versions of the activities, so, although they are similar to activities in this final version, they do not necessarily show final versions of materials, procedures, or student sheets.

Rather than emphasizing the length of a day or surface gravity of a particular planet, students use this information to answer such questions as:

Where in the solar system are there conditions favorable for life?

How did the solar system form?

How do the solar system and our planet fit in with the rest of space?

Could life exist on other planets, and if so, can we communicate with those lifeforms?

In focusing on these bigger questions and ideas, one of the end results is that the smaller facts are then endowed with more meaning.

For students who have limited background in astronomy this unit can be a good introduction to our solar system. After all, ours is the only system that has been studied closely by humans. For students with an extensive astronomical background, this unit helps to fit their understanding of the solar system into a bigger picture of the universe and gives them an opportunity to apply their knowledge to explore that popular question, "Are we alone?"

The guide uses a simulated message from extraterrestrials as a "hook" to begin the unit. In Activity 1, the students attempt to interpret a seven-part fictitious binary coded message from space. The activity serves to inspire the students to wonder about their own solar system, as well as challenge them to struggle with a mystery and express their thoughts and ideas.

In Activity 2 students analyze the light from different "stars" to explore the conditions in distant planetary systems that could possibly host life. Their study of the lifezones and lifespans of different types of stars applies to far off planetary systems as well as to our own solar system.

Activity 3 is an extended study of the solar system spread over several sessions. Students share what they already know about the solar system and do an activity to simulate how it formed. They research and prepare "planet travel brochures" and set up stations which become a part of a class tour of the solar system. They see how a small scale model of the solar system covers a vast area around their classroom.

As you will notice, throughout this guide we have generally preferred the use of the term extraterrestrial, or its popular abbreviation, ET— rather than the term alien. For one thing, this avoids confusion with the socio-political generally negative use of "illegal alien." In addition, and as part of one of the main lessons of this unit, alien is the word most often used by tabloid-style sensationalist stories that claim alien invaders have landed on Earth and make similar unsubstantiated claims. In an attempt to differentiate a scientific discussion of the possibility of life "out there," from non-scientific fictions, we think it most appropriate to refer to extraterrestrials. We are of course aware of a counter-argument, that the term alien, or outer space alien, will provoke excitement and interest among students. In a few cases, such as when students analyze a set of scientific and non-scientific articles later in the unit, we have used "alien" to provide a sense of the language most often used by both types of article.

Activity 4 gives students a chance to choose which facts about the Earth and the solar system they would communicate to any extraterrestrials who might happen to be tuning into messages from Earth.

In Activity 5 students apply information they've learned about the solar system as they design distant planetary systems that support the development of life. At the end of the activity is a critical reading assignment that could be used as homework to help students distinguish between articles based on scientific thinking and sensationalized fiction. Also included at the end of Activity 5 as a Going Further is a special mathematical activity about the probability of life existing elsewhere in the Universe, based on a series of steps often referred to as "the Drake Equation." If you have the time to present this, we would appreciate hearing your and your students' reactions. Look it over and decide whether or not to include it.

In Activity 6 the unit dovetails into language arts as students plan and write their own science fiction stories about the planetary system they have designed. This can serve as an excellent science assessment.

In addition to the wealth of astronomical concepts introduced in the unit, students also experience the process of astronomy, which is somewhat different from other sciences, in that direct experiments often cannot be used. Astronomy often involves making systematic observations, and then building mathematical, physical, or conceptual models based on the observations. These models are then tested in terms of how they predict future observations. In this unit, students research real data about stars and planetary systems, and then construct models of planetary systems consistent with this data.

By the end of the unit, the students have gained considerable knowledge about and understanding of the science of astronomy, with mathematics and language arts naturally interwoven. Most importantly, we hope this unit whets their curiosity and motivates them to ponder and pursue more and bigger questions in the future.

Whether or not the existence of extraterrestrial intelligence is confirmed any time soon, we are receiving numerous "messages from space" every day—through telescopes and information from spacecraft, and derived from our increasingly sophisticated analysis of this mass of data. The understanding your students gain in this unit can help them draw their own conclusions about the significance of these "messages from space."

"Empty space is like a kingdom, and heaven and earth no more than a single individual person in that kingdom...How unreasonable it would be to suppose that besides the heaven and earth which we can see there are no other heavens and no other earths?"

—Teng Mu, thirteenth century philosopher

Time Frame

Activity 1: Message From Space

    Session 1: Making Contact   45–60 minutes
    Session 2: Interpreting a Message From Space   45–60 minutes

Activity 2: Somewhere in the Milky Way—Star Types   45–60 minutes
         and Lifezones

Activity 3: Our Neighborhood in the Milky Way—The Solar System

    Session 1: A Swirling Cloud   45–60 minutes
    Session 2: The Solar System—Travel Brochures   45–60 minutes
    Session 3: Touring the Solar System   45–60 minutes
    Session 4: Putting the Planets in Their Places   45–60 minutes

PLEASE NOTE: The above estimates for Activity 3 do NOT include recommended time for homework and other work periods during class so student teams can have sufficient time to do quality research and work on their projects for "Touring the Solar System." Allowing such additional time is strongly recommended. Additional time can likewise be important in student creation of science fiction stories in Activity 6.

Activity 4: Dear Extraterrestrials…   45–60 minutes

Activity 5: Making a Planetary System   45–60 minutes

Activity 6: Science Fiction Stories   45–60 minutes

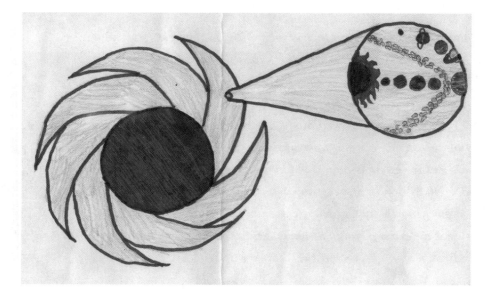

"There are some hundred billion (10^{11}) galaxies, each with, on the average, a hundred billion stars. In all the galaxies, there are perhaps as many planets as stars, 10^{11} x 10^{11} = 10^{22}, or ten billion trillion. In the face of such overpowering numbers, what is the likelihood that only one ordinary star, the Sun, is accompanied by an inhabited planet? Why should we, tucked away in some forgotten corner of the Cosmos, be so fortunate? To me, it seems far more likely that the universe is brimming over with life. But we humans do not yet know. We are just beginning our explorations. From eight billion light-years away we are hard pressed to find even the cluster in which our Milky Way Galaxy is embedded, much less the Sun or the Earth. The only planet we are sure is inhabited is a tiny speck of rock and metal, shining feebly by reflected Sunlight, and at this distance utterly lost. "

Carl Sagan, *Cosmos*

Activity 1: Message From Space

Two Session Overview

In this activity, students are introduced to the scientific search for radio signals that reach Earth, possibly from extraterrestrial civilizations. (Whether or not actual visits by extraterrestrials are plausible is discussed in Activity 2.) The idea of tuning into radio messages from intelligent life elsewhere raises questions of how we could overcome the cosmic "language barrier" and this leads the class to explore how basic mathematics can be used to translate a radio signal into a pictorial message.

The message that students receive in Session 2 of this activity is meant to spark ideas that will be addressed in future sessions in this unit. As their understanding of their own solar system and more distant star systems deepens, so may their interpretations of the message.

*You may want to point out to your students that signals, such the signals in this unit's message, or the radio signals that scientists seek to detect from outer space, are generated by **technology**, not by living beings. Scientists who search for extraterrestrial life are actually seeking evidence of the kind of technology that could generate such signals. From that evidence, it could then be inferred that beings intelligent enough to create such technology must exist. This is an important idea, because it explains the logic involved in the current scientific searches for extraterrestrial intelligence.*

Session 1: Making Contact

Overview

Imagining that they are SETI (Search for Extraterrestrial Intelligence) scientists, students listen to a series of four radio wave "messages" that might be received from space. With each, they vote whether or not they think it might be a message from extraterrestrials. They are introduced to the idea of how ETs might try to communicate using pictures and how we on Earth might mathematically decode their radio signals to reveal the pictures that they send us.

*We plan to have a series of sounds you can use in this activity available on the Internet, from the GEMS web site. Go to **www.lhs.berkeley.edu/ GEMS** and look for a "sound message from space."*

What You Need

For the class:
- ❏ items with bar codes printed on them
- ❏ *(optional)* tape player and tape recording of TV or radio static and beep patterns
- ❏ *(optional)* overhead projector and transparency of some article and/or illustration of "ETs" from the tabloids

You could show a clip from a video about Earth receiving a message from outer space, such as a brief excerpt from Contact. *Or, you could show students the overhead of a tabloid newspaper headline about outer space lifeforms.*

One teacher dialed up a fax machine from a speaker phone and recorded the signals of the fax machine trying (unsuccessfully) to communicate with a fax machine at the other end of the phone line. This produced a "hi-tech" sound that is actually a binary code, which is exactly what the signal is supposed to represent.

Brainstorm: What's in Space ?

If you have many students for whom English is a second language, or if you think your students may benefit from it, you may want to begin the unit by asking your students to brainstorm things that might be in space. This might be done as a whole class discussion, in small groups or pairs, and possibly with illustrations and books about space on hand to aid in communication.

If possible, get books and posters related to space, extraterrestrials, and communication as resources and for display in your classroom. You may also want to provide your students with opportunities to search on the Internet for information. Caution them that information on the net is not necessarily any more reliable than information from a person shouting on a street corner. We recommend the Views of the Solar System web site, with photos and information on planets at http:// spaceart.com/solar/

❏ *(optional)* VCR and video clip of message being received from *Contact, The Arrival,* or other relevant movie

For each student:
❏ 1 copy of the A Binary Message student sheet (master on page 14)

Getting Ready

1. Copy the A Binary Message student sheet (master on page 14) for each student.

2. If you can, make a tape recording of the four sounds to be used as make-believe radio signals. (These are available via the net at www.lhs.berkeley.edu/GEMS)

- The first two sounds should each be about 10 seconds of noise that sounds like radio static. To make this part of the tape, you can record yourself or you can record actual static from a radio or television that is not tuned to a broadcast signal.

- For the third sound, the pulsar, you can record yourself humming any tone getting louder and softer in a regular rhythm about once every second. Alternatively, you can record radio or television static while turning the volume up and down.

- For the fourth sound (the alleged message from extraterrestrials) you need to find or make a signal that sounds like a coded signal. Simply going "dee-dee-duh-duh-dee-duh-duh-duh-dee-dee-duh-dee..." in the style of a Morse code message is sufficient.

3. If you are not going to make the tape, practice the signals described in the "Receiving Signals" section of this activity so that you can give a live performance.

4. If you've decided to show a video clip of an extraterrestrial message being received, set up the VCR and cue the video.

What Are We Looking For?

1. Ask your students if they know any stories—from books, television, or movies—about messages from outer space extraterrestrials or about ETs that come to Earth. Allow them to share a few. Point out that these stories, wild and fantastic as they are, come from the imaginations of authors who are ordinary human beings. These authors are "Terrestrials," people from planet Earth. Explain that creatures from other parts of space are often referred to as "aliens," but more scientifically as extraterrestrials, or ETs, for short.

2. Explain that in the early 1980s some scientists began a project called SETI, which stands for **S**earch For **E**xtraterrestrial **I**ntelligence to investigate the possibility that contact with extraterrestrials may someday occur. SETI was a branch of NASA (the National Aeronautics and Space Administration, which runs the U.S. government's space program). In the 1990s government funding for SETI was cut, but SETI continues to operate with private funding.

SETI Institute

3. Let students know that SETI scientists study stars in our galaxy to try to understand which ones may be hosts to star sytems where life could possibly develop. Some SETI scientists use large radio receivers and try to "listen in" on radio signals that ETs may be sending to each other or signals they may be sending to us!

Receiving Signals

1. Ask your students to imagine that they are SETI scientists who have pointed a huge radio telescope at a cluster of stars. You will let them listen in on the signal that was received. Instruct them to vote thumbs up, if they think the signal might be a message from intelligent extraterrestrials, thumbs down if they think it is not, and thumbs to the side if they're not sure.

2. Imitate the sound of static with your voice, or play the first sound on the tape you've prepared.

3. Note their votes, and let them discuss the reasons for their choices. Tell them that scientists call a signal like this "noise." It is produced naturally by some objects in space, and no one regards it as a sign of intelligent life.

*You can easily make the sounds of the radio signals with your voice. A little practice ahead of time is all the preparation needed. **However,** teachers have found that the excitement among students is greatly increased if the signals come from a speaker and not from the teacher's mouth. Students should be aware that the signals are not really from space, but the addition of a little bit of modern technology, even if it just a cassette player, allows them to imagine more easily that they are studying real messages from space.*

4. Announce that they will hear the signal from a second star cluster. Repeat the sound of static. You should expect students to give a thumbs-down to this signal. Let students know that we expect to hear nothing but noise from most places we point our radio telescope.

5. Tell students to imagine we have pointed the dish of the radio telescope at a different star cluster and have picked up more radio waves. Make steady beeps at regular intervals (about one each second) with your voice, or play the third sound on the tape you prepared. Have them vote with their thumbs as before. Many of your students will probably vote yes.

6. Tell students this actually happened in 1967. Scientists did pick up radio waves that were regular beeps, and wondered whether they had picked up a message from ETs. They even called the sources of the signals LGMs, which stood for "little green men!" Astronomers have since learned that signals like this do not come from lifeforms, but from collapsed stars that are rapidly spinning. These stars are called *pulsars.* They are interesting objects, but they are not signs of intelligent life.

7. Tell students to imagine that we've picked up more radio waves from yet another star cluster. Make an irregular pattern of beeps that sounds somewhat like Morse code with your voice, or play the fourth sound on the tape you prepared. Tell your students to vote with their thumbs whether they think it is a message from an intelligent extraterrestrial.

8. A complex repeating signal like this sounds as if it must have been made by someone on purpose. Let them know that repeating patterns such as this are exactly what SETI scientists are searching for. They have never definitely received anything like them...so far.

What Kind Of Message?

1. Ask your students what kind of languages they think extraterrestrials might use. Explain that human languages are spoken or visual, such as sign language. Human language can be recorded in writing or pictures, on paper, on cassette tape or CD, or on computer disks. Extraterrestrial languages could be similar or completely strange to us.

Many students who have seen outer space beings depicted on TV and in movies and who have grown up surrounded by the English language may assume that extraterrestrials will speak English! You may wish to take the opportunity to ask students if any of them speak another language or have been in non-English speaking situations. Point out that there are many languages even here on Earth, and unless they have somehow been eavesdropping on English speaking human beings, extraterrestrial lifeforms would almost certainly not speak English!

2. Very briefly brainstorm different methods of communication used on Earth, by humans and other animals. Ask students how extraterrestrial lifeforms with completely different languages and methods of communication might communicate with each other.

3. Tell students that it is thought that ETs who could send us messages would have at least one thing in common with us—they must be able to send and receive radio signals. Not only are radio signals a good way to send information, radio signals are the only practical way we know of to send a message huge distances across empty space. There could be millions of interesting and highly intelligent civilizations, but if they do not send and receive radio signals they will be out of touch with us.

4. Ask students if they can think of any way to make messages that could be understood by anyone—no matter what language they speak—and that could be sent by radio waves.

5. Tell students that SETI scientists have sent one well known message into space using a mathematically coded picture to try to communicate with any lifeforms who might happen to receive the signals. A culture intelligent enough to build radio receivers may recognize the mathematical patterns and be able to decode the picture.

6. Explain that the simplest code for sending a picture by radio signals is a "binary code." A binary code has only two types of signals. They can be called by many names such as "1" and "0," "on" and "off," or "beep" and "boop." A bar code on an item from a grocery store is a binary code in which the two signals are "black" and "white."

7. You may want to show them an item with a bar code on it. Ask if there are other items in the room with bar codes. Explain that binary codes are a way to store and communicate any information. Computers work entirely in binary codes. Digital television sets receive binary signals and create a picture from binary codes.

Note: If your students suggest Morse code, point out that it is a code that can be used to communicate words in a language, but it is not a language in itself. A message can be sent in Morse code, but unless you know the language it is in, you can't understand the message.

Decoding a Practice Message

1. Tell students that a simple way to make a picture that can be turned into a binary code is by making the picture out of a rectangular grid of small squares. Each small

square piece of the picture is called a **bit** and each bit is either black or white.

2. Pass out the A Binary Message sheet to each student. Tell the students that you have a set of 80 bits, a binary code, that they must turn into a picture. You will read a list of signals in the binary message and they will fill in the grid.

3. Tell the students that the grid must be a rectangle that contains 80 squares. Ask them if there is more than one way to do this. Have them come up with a few ways. Have students choose different grids to use, and ask them to outline them on the graph paper. (Make sure that someone chooses a grid that is 16 squares across and five squares high, because that is the correct one for decoding this message—but **don't tell them this**.)

4. Students should get ready to fill in the squares from left to right, completing rows from top to bottom. A "beep" signal means to fill in the square, and a "click" signal means to leave the square blank and go on to the next. Let them know that you will read off the bits slowly and steadily and that it is very important that they keep up. One slip could spoil the whole message. Tell them that a quick scribble, or even just an "X" is enough to put into each square that gets a "beep" signal.

5. **Instruct students not to distract their classmates.** Students who think they may see the message appear may be tempted to alert their friends. They may even be tempted to ask their friends to take a look. This may cause everyone to miss a bit (or several bits) and the messages will come out wrong.

6. After answering questions, start reading the list of bits in the signal. Read one every two or three seconds, and watch the students to see how they are keeping up. (You may want to go even more slowly on the first 4 or 5, to make sure everyone understands what to do.)

7. After all the bits have been read off and the students have completed their grids, have them look at each other's grids. Those students who used the wrong grids will have a meaningless scattering of black and white. The ones who filled in a 16 x 5 grid will probably waste no time letting the others know that they got a message and their grids were the correct

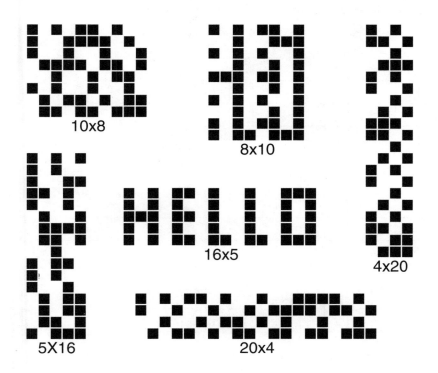

10x8

8x10

HELLO
16x5

4x20

5X16

20x4

8. Remind students that this is a message from Earthlings to Earthlings. If extraterrestrials sent a picture of one of their written words to us it would be meaningless because we would not know their language and we would not know their method of writing it down. (Again, unless they had already mastered the written English language, it wouldn't say "HELLO!" in English.)

9. Have students recall the radio signals they heard that seemed to be from intelligent extraterrestrials. Tell them to imagine that those signals have been decoded successfully into pictures—in the next session they will get a chance to figure out for themselves what that message from outer space might mean.

A BINARY MESSAGE *(From One Earthling to Another)*

1. beep	41. click		
2. click	42. click		
3. beep	43. beep		
4. beep	44. click		
5. beep	45. click		
6. beep	46. beep		
7. click	47. click		
8. beep	48. beep		
9. click	49. beep		
10. click	50. click		
11. beep	51. beep		
12. click	52. click		
13. click	53. beep		
14. beep	54. click		
15. beep	55. click		
16. beep	56. beep		
17. beep	57. click		
18. click	58. click		
19. beep	59. beep		
20. click	60. click		
21. beep	61. click		
22. click	62. beep		
23. click	63. click		
24. beep	64. beep		
25. click	65. beep		
26. click	66. click		
27. beep	67. beep		
28. click	68. click		
29. click	69. beep		
30. beep	70. beep		
31. click	71. click		
32. beep	72. beep		
33. beep	73. beep		
34. beep	74. click		
35. beep	75. beep		
36. click	76. beep		
37. beep	77. click		
38. beep	78. beep		
39. click	79. beep		
40. beep	80. beep		

1. Mark off a section of the graph paper with a rectangle that contains exactly 80 squares. Each square is for one bit (a "beep" or a "click") in the message.

2. Get ready to fill in the squares as someone reads the list of bits in the message. Start in the upper left-hand corner and move across the rectangle bit by bit. As you finish a row, move to the next row starting at the left.

3. For each bit that is a "beep" fill in the square. For each bit that is a "click" leave the square blank and move on to the next square.

4. Compare your picture to those of students who used different rectangles for their grids. Which grid is the right one for decoding the message?

Session 2: Interpreting a Message From Space

Overview

In this session students interpret a fictitious message from space. They may come up with several possible meanings for some parts of the message. There will be other parts of the message for which they may not find any meaning at all. As with any real science investigation, there is no "answer key" to say what is right and wrong. Only further investigation of the message and its source will help show which interpretations make sense. During the rest of this unit, students continue the process of interpreting the message that they began in this session.

What You Need

For the class:

- ❏ 1 overhead transparency and 1 copy of each of the seven pages of the Message from Space (masters on pages 18–24)
- ❏ 1 overhead transparency of the Grid for Message (master on page 25)
- ❏ an overhead projector
- ❏ some post-it notes for student's comments

For each team of 2–4 students:

- ❏ 1 copy of each of the seven pages of the Message from Space (masters on pages 18–24)

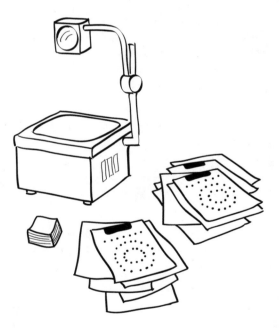

Getting Ready

1. Copy the seven pages of the Message from Space (masters on pages 18–24) for each group of students as well as a copy to post for the whole class, and make one transparency of all seven pages. Also make a transparency of the Grid for Message (master on page 25).

2. Set up the overhead projector. Place the Message from Space and Grid for Message transparencies nearby.

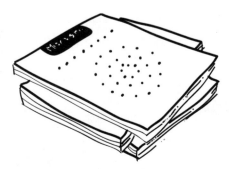

Making Contact

Optional section for students who have studied prime numbers:

The alleged extraterrestrial message is on grids that are 61 squares across by 67 squares down, for a total of 4087 squares or bits. You might give your students time to figure out what sizes of rectangular grids could accommodate this number of bits. The answer is only two. (We are not including having all the bits in a straight line as an acceptable grid.) You can point out that if ETs want us to decode their messages easily they can make the dimensions of the grid prime numbers. That gives us fewer wrong choices when we are trying to decode the message. When SETI broadcast a message into space in 1974 they used a grid that was 23 across by 73 down. This message is discussed further in Activity 4.

You don't need to overlay the grid each time.

1. If you are starting a new day with this part of the activity, remind students that the messages that they are going to see have been decoded from a binary signal. The code was allegedly received by our radio telescope from a distant cluster of stars.

2. Have your students work in groups of two to four. Let them know that it's their job to try to figure out the meaning of the seven pages of the message. Pass out one copy of the first page to each small group, and have them begin interpreting and discussing it within their group. Give them two or three minutes of discussion time.

3. Place the transparency of the first page of the message on the overhead, and draw your students' attention to it. Lay the transparency of the Grid for Message on top of it to remind them that each black space and each white space is a little piece, or bit, of the picture. Then remove the grid. Ask them to share their interpretations with the whole class. Accept all serious ideas and encourage discussion and debate.

4. Continue this same process with each page of the message; handing out the page, allowing the groups time for discussion, then sharing ideas with the whole class with the appropriate page on the overhead. Keep the pace fast, allowing approximately two minutes for small group discussion of each page. You may want to hand out pages 5 and 6 together, and discuss them simultaneously. Encourage students to lay the pages out in sequence in front of them.

5. Point out any portions of the message your students have not explained yet, and challenge them to continue to try to interpret all parts of the message. Tell them that you will leave the seven pages of the message posted in a prominent location throughout the unit, and that they may write their explanations on post-its next to each page, if they choose.

6. Tell them that if a message were actually received from an extraterrestrial civilization, no one on Earth would know for certain what they intended to communicate. If this were to happen in real life, there would be no way to know if any particular interpretation was correct or not. Let them know that with this simulated message the same will be true, and that they will never be told the exact intended meaning of the message.

7. Encourage your students to keep their eyes and ears open to the news in the future, because a message like this one might be received in real life.

If there is time you can begin the first part of the next activity, a simulated look at the sky, which also uses the overhead projector.

Just for the Teacher:

Certain parts of this message are intended to have a meaning that the students should either recognize during this activity, or sometime during future sessions in this unit. **Avoid telling them the intended meanings even if students never come up with them themselves. It is important that students realize that the "right answer" is not always available to scientists and that whatever ideas they do have about the message must come from *themselves* and not be given to them.**

Nevertheless, teachers may find it helpful to know how the intended meaning of the message fits into the rest of this unit.

Page 1 of the message shows the formation of the star system where the extraterrestrial life began. It is similar to the pepper and water simulation that students conduct at the beginning of Activity 3.

Page 2 of the message simply shows the extraterrestrial star system.

Page 3 shows one planet marked as the one that the ETs originally inhabit, and page 4 shows the planets that the ETs colonize. When students design their distant planetary systems in Activity 5, they may relate these pages to the concept of star lifezones, which they explore in Activity 2.

Page 5 and page 6 suggest some change or catastrophe that befalls the ETs' original planet. Whether it is a natural change, or a consequence of their development, is not specified.

Page 7 shows the positions of their star system and our solar system in the Milky Way Galaxy. This implies that the ETs know about us and this message is intended especially for us.

At the top of page 1 there is a list of symbols that represent the numerals 0 to 9. This counting system is used in several ways. It is used to number each page. It is used to show the passing of time on pages 2 to 6. On page 7 the planets are numbered, and the system is used to show how many times the distance from the Sun to the Earth their planetary system is from ours. Most of the parts of the message that use the numbering system will probably remain mysterious to your students. That is okay.

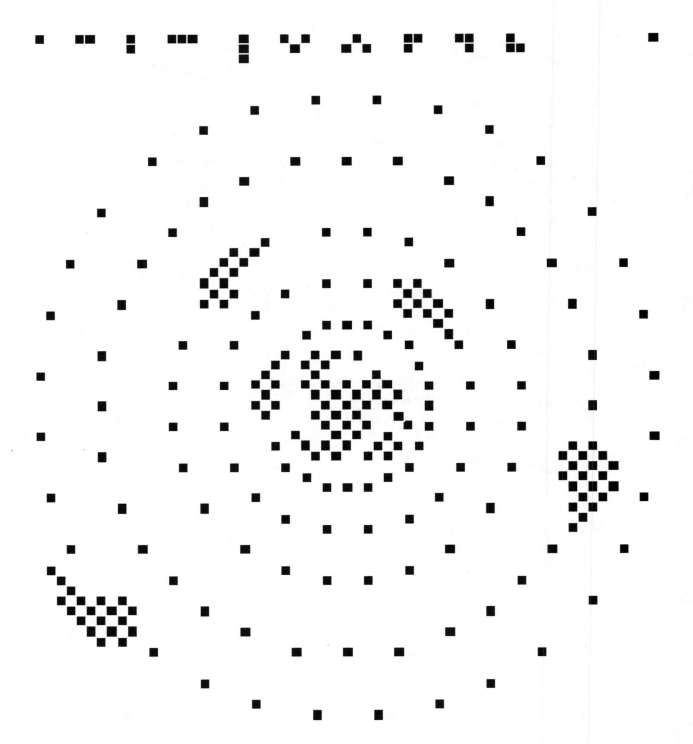

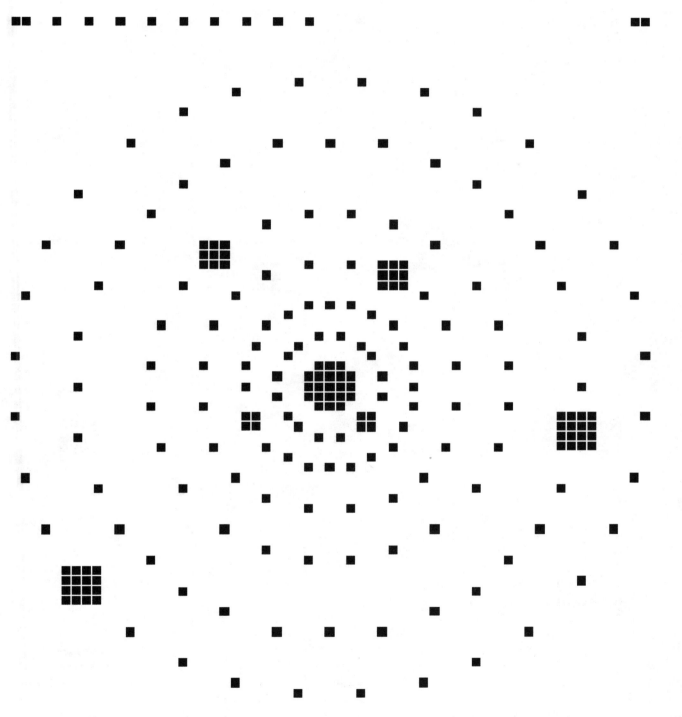

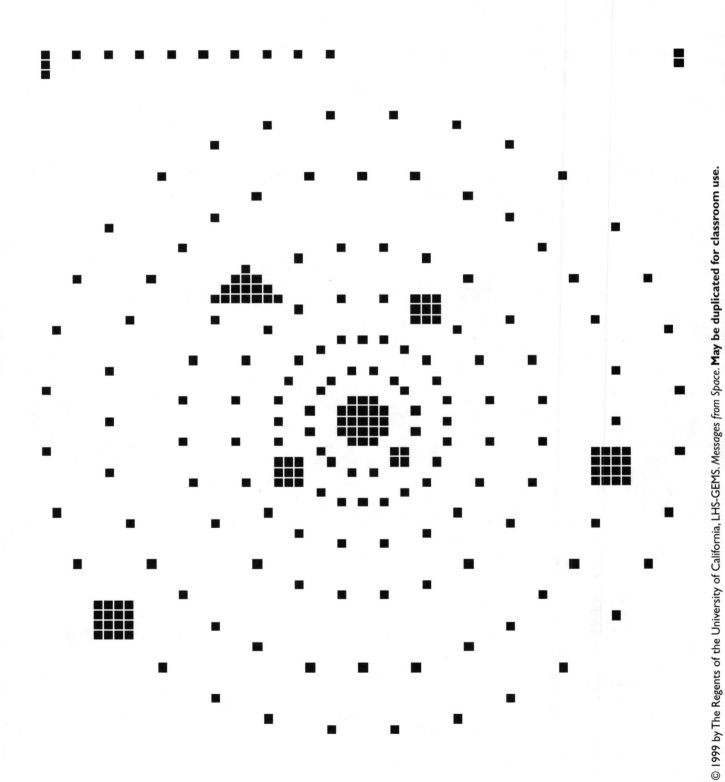

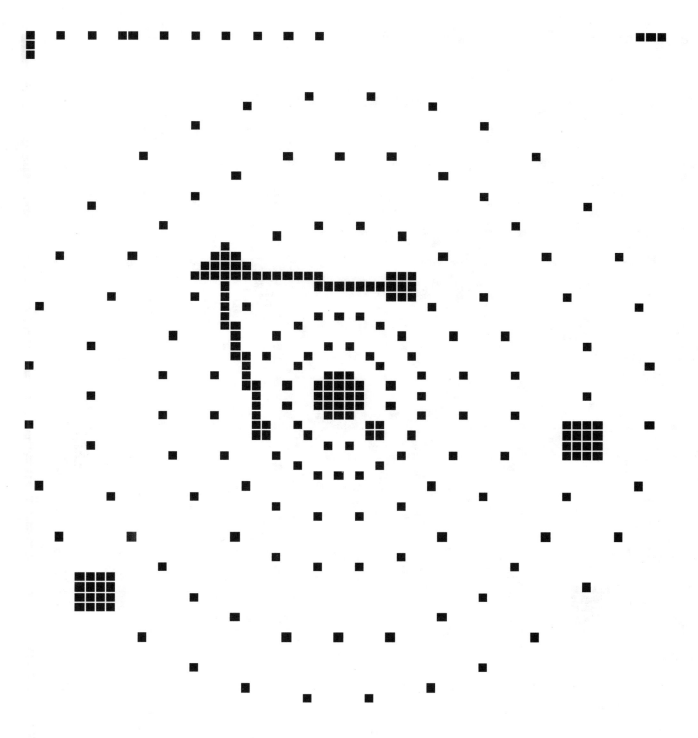

PAGE 5

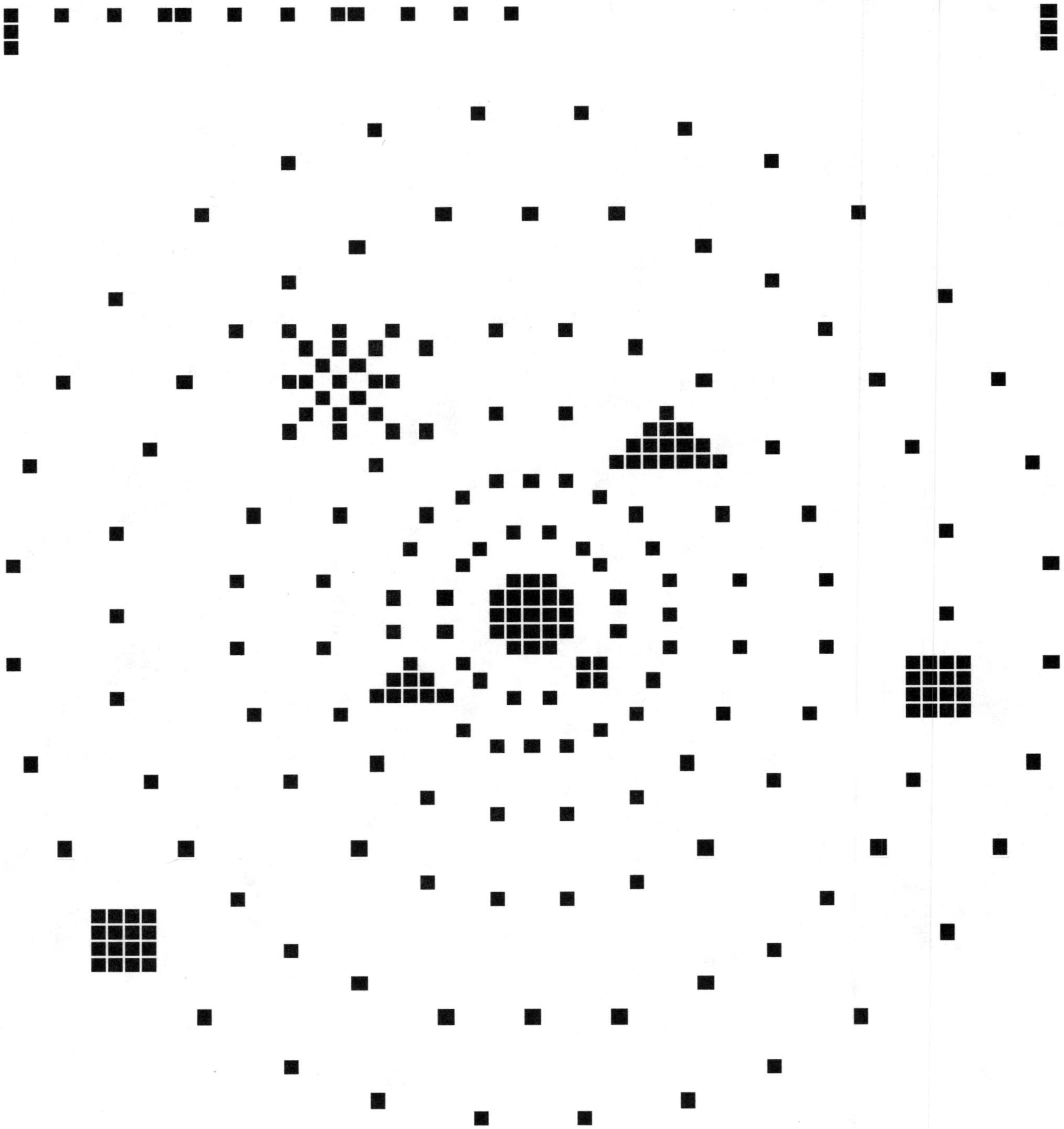

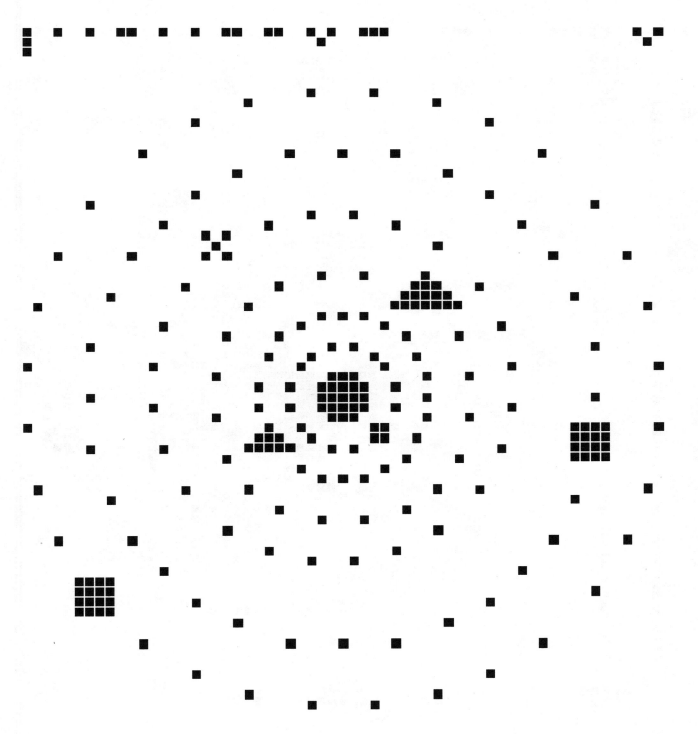

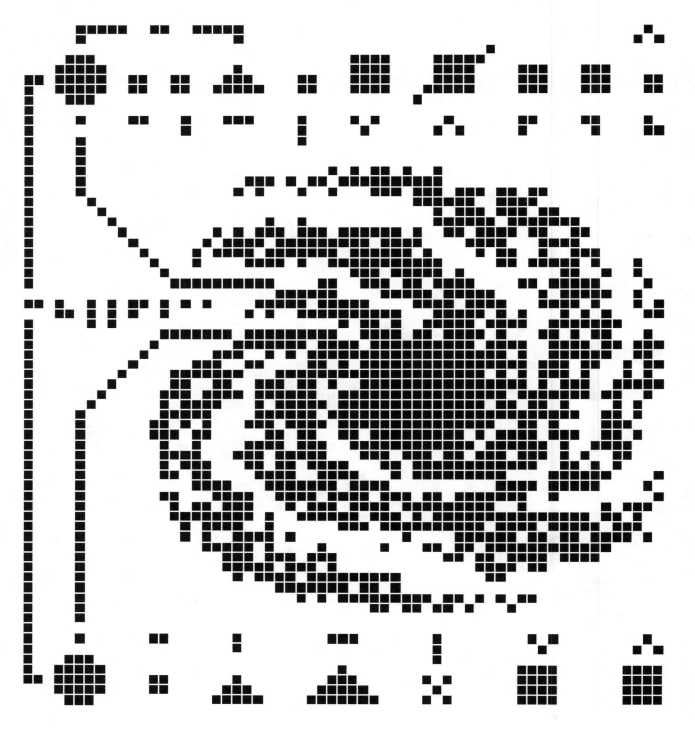

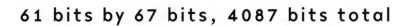

61 bits by 67 bits, 4087 bits total

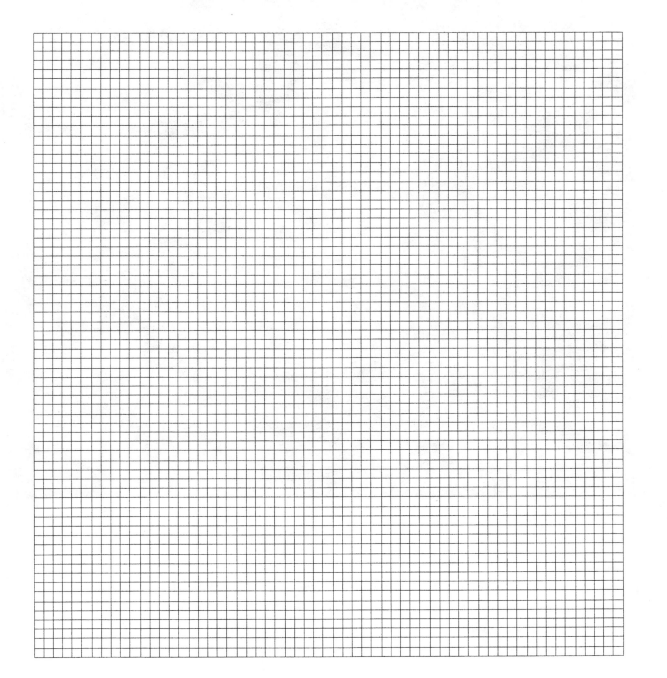

"A handful of sand contains about 10,000 grains, more than the number of stars we can see with the naked eye on a clear night. But the number of stars we can see is only the tiniest fraction of the number of stars that are. What we see at night is the merest smattering of the nearest stars. Meanwhile the Cosmos is rich beyond measure: the total number of stars in the universe is greater than all the grains of sand on all the beaches of the planet Earth."

Carl Sagan, *Cosmos*

Activity 2: Somewhere in the Milky Way—Star Types and Lifezones

Overview

An overhead projector "planetarium show" gives students a "cosmological geography" experience that highlights the multitude of stars and the vastness of space. As they explore the heavens via a series of transparencies, they see that even the "nearest" star clusters are remote enough to make the idea of a visit from extraterrestrials almost unthinkable.

Then the class narrows in on the stars in the part of the galaxy from which the radio "message" came. Students are introduced to the concept of a lifezone—the area around a star where liquid water might be found. Four different light bulbs are used to represent different types of stars. Students use radiometers to study the illumination of each of the stars and determine the boundaries of each star's lifezone. A simpler alternative investigation is included for classes that cannot obtain radiometers. Please see Planning Your Teams in the "Getting Ready" section below for more about the alternative, and the "Behind the Scenes" section for more about radiometers.

See the end of the "Resources" section, page 156, for instructions on how to make your own radiometer.

The session ends with a simulation of the lifespans of the four different types of stars. Two of the stars "burn out" very quickly as the students watch, but they find that one star is still shining when they return the next day. If possible, avoid starting this simulation on a Friday or on the day before a vacation. See the note on page 37 if your situation makes this simulation logistically difficult.

For more on star types and life spans, see "Behind the Scenes," starting on page 135. There is also a great deal of information on the stars, and many beautiful galactic images, on the world wide web.

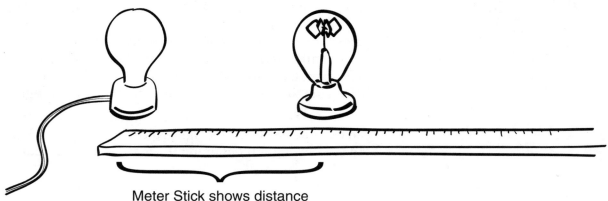

Meter Stick shows distance
from the "star" to the radiometer.

What You Need

For the class:

- ❐ 4 sockets
- ❐ extension cords as necessary
- ❐ 8–16 meter sticks with centimeter markings
- ❐ 4 light bulbs (See "Getting Ready" for details.)
- ❐ an overhead projector
- ❐ 1 overhead transparency each of A Spiral Galaxy, Many Galaxies, Star Cluster the Message Came From, and Our Solar System (masters on pages 41–44)
- ❐ butcher paper for the Star Types chart
- ❐ 3 permanent markers: 1 each yellow, red, and blue
- ❐ a clock with a second hand

For each team of 2–4 students:

- ❐ 1 radiometer
- ❐ 1 copy of the Star Types and Lifezones data sheet (master on page 39)
- ❐ 1 copy of the Feeling The Heat data sheet (master on page 40; use this instead of or in addition to the Star Types and Lifezones data sheet. See "Getting Ready" for details.)

Getting Ready

1. Planning Your Teams

How you divide your students into teams may depend on how many radiometers you can obtain. Ideally you should have one radiometer for each group. There is an alternative investigation (see "Feeling the Heat" on page 35) that uses no radiometers at all, although it is not as dramatic. You also have the option of doing both investigations, with half the teams using radiometers and half doing the alternative activity, and then switching.

In a class with fewer than 25 students, the activities can be done around three light bulbs. Consider leaving out the blue light if obtaining the materials for all four is difficult.

2. Prepare the Overhead Transparencies

a. Make one overhead transparency each of A Spiral Galaxy, Many Galaxies, Star Cluster the Message Came From, and Our Solar System (masters on pages 41–44).

b. On the Star Cluster the Message Came From transparency, use a permanent marker to lightly color in the stars yellow, red, or blue as indicated below.

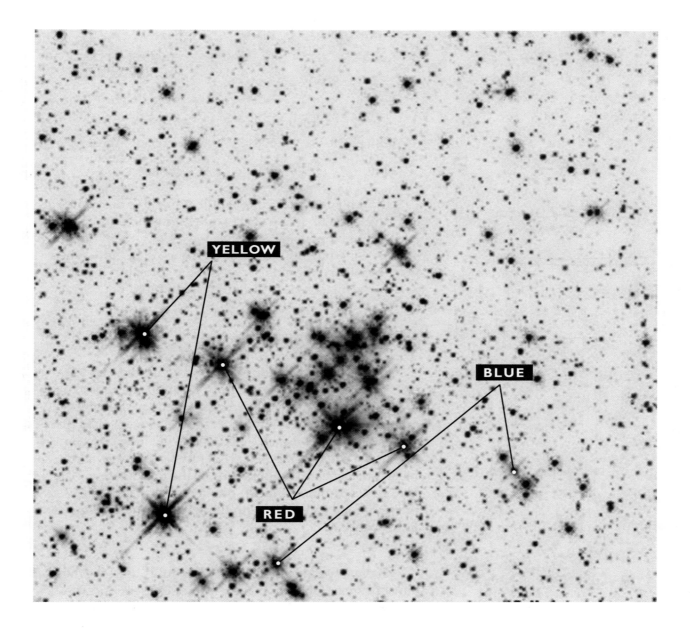

3. Prepare the Light Bulbs

You will need four light bulbs gradated in terms of wattage, size, and color.

The smallest size and smallest wattage = red
Next smallest size and wattage = yellow
The second largest size and wattage = white
The largest size and wattage = blue

If you can't find a certain color of light bulb, you can color a white one with a permanent marker.

Example:

Color	Watts	Size
red	15–25	smallest (appliance or decorative bulb)
yellow	60	next smallest (stan dard size bug-light)
white	100	second largest
blue	200	largest

Do not attempt to color a bulb while it is hot. After coloring, screw it into a socket, plug it in and allow it to remain lit before using it in the classroom. It may smoke slightly for a few minutes, but then should be fine. When lit, students will be able to discern the color, but it will not be as colorful as a store-bought colored bulb.

4. Prepare the Workspaces

Screw each of the four light bulbs into the four sockets. Place the four sockets in four locations of your classroom with a full meter of workspace on one side of the bulb. If you have a full meter on both sides, you can place two meter sticks by each bulb. This will allow two teams to work at each light bulb. Students should not wield meter sticks near the light bulbs or the radiometers. The meter stick should be taped down on the work surface so that their ends are even with the center of the bulb in the light socket.

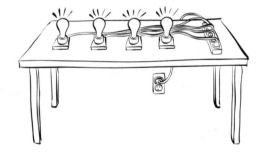

Have a space ready for the light bulbs used for the Star Lifespan Simulation at the end of the session. These should be in a location where all students can see them from their seats. Having the bulbs on a shelf or counter under the Star Types chart is preferable. See the note near the Star Lifespan Simulation instructions (page 37) for an option in case your situation makes this simulation difficult.

5. **Make the Star Types Chart**

Make the following chart on butcher paper or the chalkboard. Include spaces for all four types of stars (light bulbs). The chart will need to remain visible for the remainder of the unit. You may want to color in the circles representing the four star types with the corresponding colors.

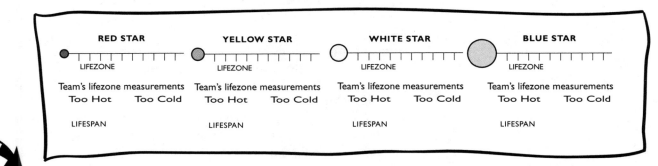

Where Did the Message Come From?

1. Invite students to go on a simulated stargazing session to search for the source of the radio signals that carried the message. Show the transparency A Spiral Galaxy. Explain that it is a grouping of many billions of stars. Have them describe some of the shapes and structures they see.

2. Tell students we live in a galaxy that is probably much like the one shown. It is called the Milky Way. Ask them why we can never see the Milky Way Galaxy in a photograph like the one shown. [Since we see the Milky Way from the inside, the stars of the Milky Way are all around us.] Explain that, since the Milky Way is flat (something like a pancake) the thickest part of the Milky Way appears, from Earth, as a band of stars across the sky. On a very clear, dark night this band of stars gives the sky a "milky" look because the stars are too far away for us to make them out individually. Every star we can see in the sky is part of the Milky Way Galaxy, but the particularly "milky" looking band of stars is also called the Milky Way. Ask students if they have seen this Milky Way and find out where they were when they saw it.

3. Show the transparency Many Galaxies. Explain that beyond the Milky Way Galaxy there are billions of other galaxies. Whichever way a telescope points there are galax-

ies to be seen, although not all telescopes are powerful enough to see them. So far, SETI scientists have only occasionally considered sending signals to other galaxies. They are so far away it would take a radio signal over two million years to reach the next nearest major galaxy to the Milky Way.

4. Show the transparency Star Cluster the Message Came From. Tell students that within our own Milky Way Galaxy there are 400–500 billion stars, so there is plenty of territory for SETI scientists to explore. Ask students to suppose they had a spaceship that could explore the area around one star **every minute.** Of course that speed is absurd, but even then, it would take the spaceship nearly a million years to explore every star in the galaxy! Such a spaceship could not exist, because it takes light about 100,000 years to cross the galaxy, and the travel time for any spaceship would be much longer. Let students know that the point is **the distances involved are immense!** That is why SETI scientists, at this point, explore the possibility of sending signals, **not** the possibility of making visits— neither visits to extraterrestrials nor visits from them!

5. This is a good time to stop for questions. You may want to respond to some questions yourself or you may list some questions for the class for further study. With regard to the impossibility of travel between distant stars, students may have heard stories of "worm holes," "warp speed," or "suspended animation" that they will want to discuss. While some of these ideas derive from science fiction, acknowledge that what may seem impossible now may one day be possible as new discoveries are made. SETI scientists are certainly open to new discoveries. That's what the project is all about. They can't predict what the new discoveries will be, but, at least for now, interstellar travel has been ruled out.

Lifezones

1. Tell your students the part of the sky that you are displaying on the overhead contains the cluster of stars from which the message allegedly came. Point out the cluster and note that all the stars are not the same. Ask them what differences they notice among them. They may mention size and shape. If they do not mention color, then draw it to their attention. Ask them to come forward and point out on the screen any stars that appear to have color.

2. Tell your students that temperature determines the color of a star, and stars are classified into seven different types: blue, blue white, white, yellow white, yellow, orange, and red. Ask what color star they think our Sun is, then tell them that it is classified as a yellow star. The hottest stars are the bluest, and the least hot stars are the reddest. Avoid saying that the red stars are cool or cold. They are hot! (Just less hot than the others.)

3. Tell your students that they don't know which of these stars the message came from. Let them know they will be studying examples of each type of star to try to understand which kind of star is most likely to be the kind from which the message could come. It must be a star that could have the kind of planet that intelligent living creatures could live on.

4. Let your students know that no one knows what life in other parts of the galaxy would be like. It might be too large, too small, or too different for us to recognize. For this exercise we will look for places that could support **Earthlike** life.

5. Ask your students what kinds of things a planet would have to have to support life, Earthlike life. (A poster of Earth from space gives good visual clues about what Earth has that supports life.) List and discuss their ideas. Make sure that water is on the list. Note that Earth has water in the form of ice, vapor, and clouds, but it is the liquid form that makes life—as we know it—possible.

6. Tell them that they will be researching the zones around stars where liquid water may exist, because water is so important to life as we know it. Let them know that the area of space around a star where liquid water can exist is referred to as the *lifezone*.

7. Show the transparency of Our Solar System. Ask your students where they think there might be liquid water within our solar system. Explain that scientists believe that Venus, Earth, and Mars have all had liquid water at one time, but that Earth is the only one that they think does at the present.

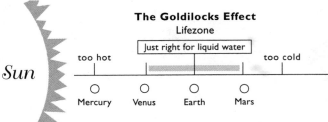

8. Let them know that the surface of Venus is too hot for liquid water although there are clouds and water vapor high in its atmosphere. The surface of Mars is too cold for anything but ice, but there seem to be dry river beds and evidence of flooding that happened long ago. The lifezone

Scientists have suspected that Europa, one of Jupiter's moons, has oceans of liquid water beneath a thick layer of ice. Pictures from the Galileo Probe support this idea. The energy that heats Europa enough to melt its ice does not come from the Sun. It comes from the gravity of Jupiter which pulls and stretches Europa to make rising and falling tides which melt the ice through friction. This is a case where liquid water could exist outside a star's traditional lifezone. For a lot more on the characteristics of Jupiter's moons, and how Galileo first observed them, we recommend the GEMS guide Moons of Jupiter.

of our Sun is the region between Venus and Mars, where it is not too hot, and not too cold. (You may want to mention that this is sometimes called "the Goldilocks Effect," in that our planet is "not too hot, not too cold—it is just right"—for life!)

9. Turn on the light bulbs in the room and explain that they will represent stars. Tell students that they'll work in teams and visit all the different types of stars to take measurements that will show them where the lifezones of these stars are.

Lifezone Measurement (for classes using radiometers)

1. Show your students a radiometer and how it spins in the sunshine or in the light of a bright lamp. The radiometer is responding to the heating effects of the light. Explain that they will use the radiometers to make the measurements that will show where the lifezones are around different types of stars.

2. Tell students that sometimes they will have to stop the vanes from turning. Show them how to "put on the brakes" by tipping the radiometer slightly.

3. Pass out the Star Types and Lifezones data sheet to each team. Go over the instructions on the data sheet for finding the outer edge and the inner edge of the lifezones. Let students know that they'll go through this same procedure for each of the four light bulbs.

4. Draw students' attention to the clock with the second hand that they can use to time the rotation of the radiometers.

5. Show students how the meter sticks are already taped down in place by each light bulb, and point out that they're aligned to measure from the center of the base of the bulb holder. Let them know that they will then measure to the center of the base of the radiometer.

6. Post and point out the Star Types chart for the class. Tell them they will have a team member add their data to the chart. Measurements should be made to the nearest centimeter.

7. **Go over safety rules.** Students must work calmly. (Self-discipline and cooperation are important on any space mission!) The simulated stars are genuinely hot and must never be touched. The light bulbs and especially the radiometers are fragile and must be treated carefully. The light bulbs are never to be moved during the activity, and the radiometers may be moved by only one person at a time. Team members should rotate the task of moving the radiometer.

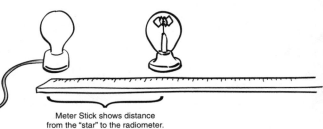

Meter Stick shows distance
from the "star" to the radiometer.

8. If you have enough radiometers for all your teams, pass them out and let the teams begin. If you have radiometers for only half your teams, go over the Feeling the Heat section which follows. Have half your teams do each of the investigations and then switch.

Feeling the Heat (lifezone activity NOT using radiometers)

1. Tell your students that they will investigate the energy from the light bulbs by seeing how it heats up their hands. Pass out the Feeling The Heat data sheets.

2. Advise students that at no time should they touch any of the light bulbs. Even a light that has been turned off might be hot enough to burn.

3. Demonstrate how to hold a hand with palm turned away from the star about 1 meter away, and slowly start to move it towards the star. Tell them to stop their hand as soon as they feel the slightest amount of warmth from the star.

4. Tell them to then record on their data sheet the distance of their hand from the star in centimeters. Say that each team member should do this a few times, to be sure.

5. Suggest they try doing it with their eyes closed. A team member should act as safety monitor to warn the person with closed eyes about getting too close to the light bulb.

6. Tell them to perform this same test on each of the four star types.

7. If you are doing this activity as a substitute for the activity with radiometers, tell the students that this measurement shows how far the lifezone extends from the star

(the outer edge of the lifezone, but not the inner edge of the lifezone where it gets too hot). Have them write the team average on the Star Types chart.

Discussion of Results

1. Move the four bulbs to the front of the classroom. Be gentle, as the filaments may break if jostled when hot. Ideally, each should be placed on a counter or shelf just below its position on the Star Types chart. They will need to be plugged in for the Star Lifespan Simulation.

2. Draw the students' attention to the results on the Star Types chart. Tell your students that the area between where it's not too hot and not too cold for liquid water is what you'll call the lifezone.

3. Do a quick and rough estimated average of each "too hot" and "too cold" result yourself, have students do it, or have them calculate the exact average for each star. (If you did Feeling The Heat as a substitute for the activity with radiometers, then you will have only the outer edge of the lifezone for each star to average and record.)

4. As you determine the averages, plot these on the segmented line next to the drawing of the star. Draw a line between the two points to indicate the lifezone for that type of star.

5. Draw a few dots to represent planets in and out of each stars' lifezone, and remind your students that planets within the zone may have liquid water and are more likely to evolve life as we know it. Remind them that those dots (planets) outside of the lifezone probably would not have liquid water, and would be unlikely to evolve life as we know it.

6. Ask your students which stars have the largest and smallest lifezone. Point out that the larger the lifezone, the greater the chance that it might have a stable planet within the lifezone that could support life.

Star Lifespan Simulation

1. Tell students that to determine which type of star would be most likely to have a planet that could evolve and support intelligent life, they not only need to take the size of lifezone into account, but also the *lifespan* of the type of star.

2. Explain that scientists now think it took over 4 billion years for intelligent life to evolve on Earth. Although we don't know if intelligent life might take more or less time to evolve on other planets, Earth is the only real example we have. If a star has suitable planets within a lifezone but the star dies too quickly, then intelligent life would not have a chance to evolve.

3. Ask your students to imagine that each second is a million years. Tell them that you will unplug each star as its time comes up.

4. Choose a clock or watch to use. Have the class say "start" when the second hand reaches an agreed upon position. Turn on all the light bulbs and announce that four new stars have been born.

5. Announce out loud, and write the actual times of "death" (the lifespan) on the Star Types chart as you turn out each light. The timing for turning off each light is as follows:

Note: The Star Lifespan Simulation helps dramatize the important concept that stars have lifespans and that different types of stars have different lifespans. We recommend that you do it if practical. Some teachers choose not to present it due to time constraints, or because, especially in middle school, it is difficult to keep the same set-up from day to day. If that is your situation, you may want to adapt or shorten the demonstration, but make sure students are aware that different kinds of stars have different lifespans and that this can affect the possibility of life arising on a planet of that star system. Because the evolution of intelligent life takes time (an estimated 4 billion years on our planet!) star lifespans are important. You will want to convey the estimates of the lifespans for the four types of stars, as shown in the table below; students build on this knowledge later in the unit.

Star	Simulation Lifespan	Actual Lifespan
blue star	10 seconds	10 million years
white star	3 minutes 20 seconds	200 million years
yellow star	2 hours 45 minutes	10 billion years
red star	28 hours (1 day is close enough)	100 billion years

6. Be quick with the blue star.

7. After the blue and white stars have both "died," tell your students to predict when the remaining two stars will each "die," or adjust any predictions they may have already made.

8. Remind them that our star, the Sun, is a yellow star. Let them know that if they are not in the room at the time of "death" of the yellow star, it will be written on the chart so they can compare it later with their prediction.

9. If the students will still be in class when the yellow star dies, make a note of the time when you will have to pull the plug on it. If not, simply turn out the lights and write the lifespan of the yellow star on the chart.

10. Make sure that the red star is shining when your students return to class the next day. At about the same time as the red star was born the day before, or a little later, turn it out, and enter the lifespan of the last surviving star—the red star—on the chart.

Going Further

Temperature and Star Color Demonstration

An unfrosted incandescent light bulb can be used to demonstrate the relationship between color and temperature. You will need a dimmer to do it. Hardware stores have dimmers that screw directly into a light socket, letting you use the dimmer in any standard fixture. The demonstration works best in a dark room.

Show the bulb at full brightness to your students, and explain that it glows because it is hot, just like a star. Have them describe the color of the glowing filament. It should be yellowish white.

Turn down the dimmer and tell the students you are turning down the electricity which makes the bulb less hot, similar to a star which has a lower surface temperature. Turn the bulb down until the light is more yellow, and have them describe the change that they see in the color of the light.

Keep turning down the bulb and have them note how it becomes more orange as the electricity is reduced and the light is less and less hot. Just before the light stops glowing it will look red.

STAR TYPES AND LIFEZONES

Too Cold: The radiometer is outside the lifezone if it takes more than 2 seconds for the vanes to spin around once.

1. Put the radiometer far enough away from the star so that the vanes do not turn.

2. Move the radiometer closer to the star until the vanes start to turn. Let them pick up speed until they are turning steadily.

3. Count 10 spins while someone on your team is watching the clock.

> If it took **more** than 20 seconds to make 10 full turns, move the radiometer **closer** to the star and try again.

> If it took **less** than 20 seconds to make 10 full turns, move the radiometer **away** from the star and try again.

When your radiometer turns steadily 10 times in 20 seconds, you are at the outer edge of the lifezone. Measure from the center of the base of the light to the center of the base of the radiometer in centimeters and write it down on the chart.

Too Hot: The radiometer is too close to the star if it takes less than 1 second for the vanes to spin around once.

1. Put the radiometer at the outer edge of the lifezone as determined above.

2. Move the radiometer closer to the star so that the vanes get a little faster. Let them pick up speed until they are turning steadily.

3. Count 10 spins while someone on your team is watching the clock.

> If it took **more** than 10 seconds to make 10 full turns, move the radiometer **closer** to the star and try again.

> If it took **less** than 10 seconds to make 10 full turns, move the radiometer **away** from the star and try again.

When your radiometer turns steadily 10 times in 10 seconds, you are at the inner edge of the lifezone. Measure from the center of the base of the light to the center of the base of the radiometer in centimeters and write it down on the chart

	TOO COLD	TOO HOT
Star Color Outer	EDGE OF LIFEZONE	INNER EDGE OF LIFEZONE
RED		
YELLOW		
WHITE		
BLUE		

© 1999 by The Regents of the University of California, LHS-GEMS. *Messages from Space.* **May be duplicated for classroom use.**

Names: _____

_____

FEELING THE HEAT

Have each team member follow the instructions below.

1. With your palm turned away from the star, start with your hand about 1 meter away from it.

2. Slowly move your hand towards the star. When you first begin to feel the smallest amount of warmth from the star, stop your hand.

3. Measure the distance from the star to your hand to the nearest centimeter.

4. Do this a few times, to be sure. You may want to try doing it with your eyes closed.

5. Write down your final measurement on the chart.

RED STAR	YELLOW STAR	WHITE STAR	BLUE STAR
I began to feel the heat at this distance:	I began to feel the heat at this distance:	I began to feel the heat at this distance:	I began to feel the heat at this distance:
Individual results	**Individual results**	**Individual results**	**Individual results**
Team average	**Team average**	**Team average**	**Team average**

A Spiral Galaxy

MANY GALAXIES

Star Cluster the Message Came From

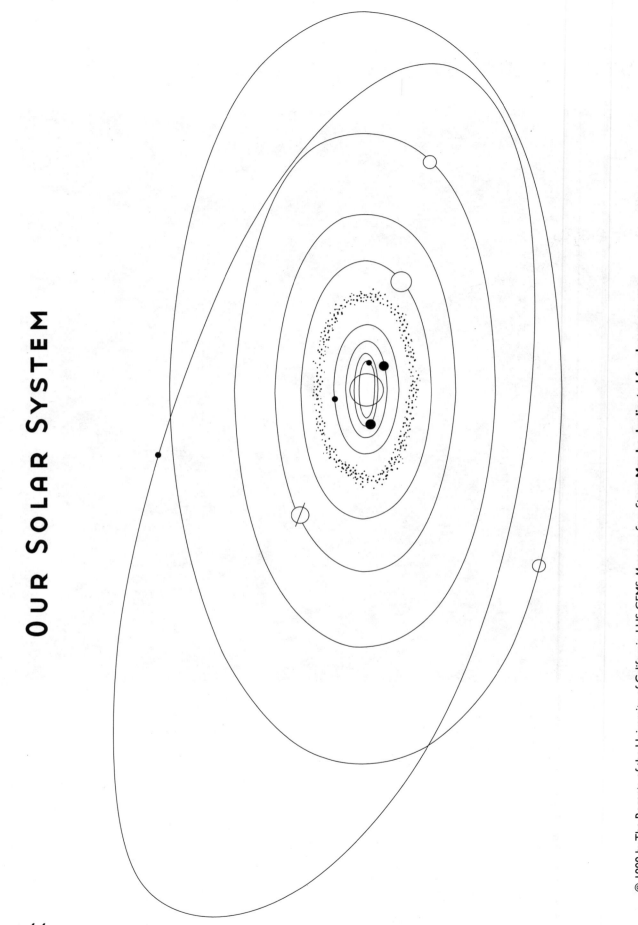

OUR SOLAR SYSTEM

Planetary Verses *by L. B.*

I love the planets in all their splendor
They whirl elliptical in Milky Way
The Sun, resplendent at their center,
Gives us heat energy, lights up our day.

Mercury, the smallest and the closest to the Sun
Mercury, the god, of course, was the fastest one.

Venus, love goddess, shrouded in mist
Beneath evening star, many lips have been kissed.

Earth—wondrous mother of life itself
From molten core to continental shelf.

Mars, named for the god of war,
Red rusty surface, with iron at core.

The prize to Jupiter for immensity
Red Spot a storm of great intensity.

Wondrous amazement the sight of Saturn brings,
Famous for its necklace of at least 10,000 rings!

Uranus's axis, near-horizontal, spins
Fifteen moons, eleven rings, very rapid winds.

Neptune with his trident, ruler of the sea—
The planet is a cold one, way too cold for you or me.

Pluto of the Underworld, sits upon his throne.
Rocky icy outpost on the edge of the unknown.

They rotate and revolve, spinning tops through space,
Orbit in a spiral dance of such amazing grace.

I love the planets in all their splendor
They whirl elliptical in Milky Way
The Sun, resplendent at their center
Gives us heat energy, lights up our day.

Activity 3: Our Neighborhood in the Milky Way— The Solar System

Four Session Overview

This section of the unit provides a chance for students to start from their current knowledge and understanding of the solar system and build from there. They are asked to consider the things they know and learn about the solar system in the context of life and the conditions under which it can survive.

The first session deals with the formation of the solar system, while the second and the third deal with the various objects (planets, moons, etc.) in the solar system. The fourth session explores the relative sizes of and distances between the planets.

While students do compile and discuss a great deal of specific planetary information, they do so within the larger context already established in the unit, keeping in mind questions such as: How did our solar system form? Where in our solar system are there conditions favorable for life? How do our solar system and our planet fit in with the rest of space? Could life exist on other planets, and if so, can we communicate with those lifeforms?

See "Behind the Scenes," on page 133 and the next several pages for more on solar system formation and the "Big Bang."

Session 1: A Swirling Cloud

Overview

In this session, the students begin by sharing what they already know about the solar system and expressing their own explanations for how it may have formed.

Students then perform a simulation of the formation of the solar system using pepper and water. This simulation shows how a disorderly collection of pepper grains in water can evolve into an orderly system that in some ways resembles a solar system. The pepper-water system does not demonstrate or explain all the reasons that a solar system forms the way it does, but students will observe that the behavior of the pepper-water system mimics the solar system in some very important ways:

- Most of the matter in the solar system clumped together in the center to form the Sun.

For more about the formation of our universe and the search for other planetary systems, visit the ORIGINS web page at http:// origins.stsci.edu

- The planets all circle the Sun in the same direction in orbits that are nearly circular.
- The orbits of the planets lie nearly in the same plane.

Although many students know these facts, even older students sometimes carry misconceptions about the structure of the solar system. The concept of a star's lifezone is confusing when these facts are misunderstood.

This session may go very quickly, especially with older students. The extra time is a good chance to revisit the Message from Space from Activity 1, Session 2. The first page of the message shows the formation of a star and planets similar to what they see in the simulation. (Resist any temptation to give inappropriate hints about this, let it come from your students.) You may also consider using the extra time to begin the introduction to Session 2 of this activity.

What You Need

For the class:

- ❑ an overhead projector
- ❑ the transparency of Our Solar System (from the previous activity)
- ❑ water
- ❑ finely ground pepper in a shaker
- ❑ *(optional)* a poster of the solar system

For each team of 2–4 students:

- ❑ 1 flat-bottomed container 3"–5" across (a bowl or a cottage cheese container works well)
- ❑ 1 stirring implement, such as a popsicle stick or a spoon
- ❑ *(optional)* finely ground pepper in a shaker, if students will be adding their own pepper

Getting Ready

1. Have the transparency of Our Solar System, from the previous activity, ready to use.

2. Fill the containers with 1" to 1 ½" of water.

What We Know

1. Tell students that the focus will now shift from the distant location where the message allegedly originated to our own solar system. Ours is the only planetary system that has been studied closely, and many ideas we come up with about another planetary system will be based on what we know about our own. Learning more about our solar system may also help us further interpret the message.

2. Show students the Our Solar System overhead transparency and/or a poster of the solar system. Tell them to take turns for a couple of minutes sharing with a partner what they think they know about the solar system. Then, ask them to share some of their ideas with the whole class. Use the overhead transparency or poster to point out features as they are discussed.

3. During the discussion, you may choose to restrict the discussion to the information your students bring up. Alternatively, you may also choose to supplement their knowledge with some of the following information:

- There are nine known planets: Mercury, Venus, Earth, Mars, Jupiter, Saturn, Uranus, Neptune, and Pluto.

- There is an asteroid belt between Mars and Jupiter. Scientists have found other objects like asteroids in a belt beyond Pluto. Some think Pluto is not a planet, but a large asteroid from that belt.

- Except for Pluto, the planets lie essentially on the same plane. The orbits of Pluto, some asteroids, and most Oort Cloud comets are in different planes.

- Except for Pluto, the orbits of the planets are nearly circular. Pluto's orbit is more oval, occasionally bringing it closer to the Sun than Neptune.

- All the planets circle the Sun in the same direction— counterclockwise, if viewed from above the North pole.

- The four planets closest to the Sun (Mercury, Venus, Earth, and Mars) are all rocky planets, and are called the terrestrial planets.

*Many students have heard that a tenth planet, "Planet X," has been discovered. It is called "Planet X" because it has **not** been discovered. The recent discoveries of planets orbiting other stars adds to the confusion, as do the occasional discoveries of strange, large asteroids that are not quite big enough to rate the title of "planet." As of 1999 there were still only **nine** known planets in our solar system.*

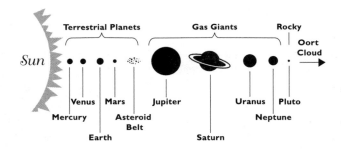

- The four planets beyond Mars (Jupiter, Saturn, Uranus and Neptune) all have solid cores covered by huge cold atmospheres of gases, and are called the gas giants. They are much farther apart than the rocky planets.

- No one knows why Pluto, a very small rocky and icy planet, is just beyond the gas giant zone.

- It is generally accepted that our Sun is also surrounded by a vast cloud of comets (the Oort cloud). Most of these comets are far beyond the orbit of Pluto.

4. You may want to mention that scientists estimate that it took about 100 million years for the solar system to form. No one knows exactly how it formed, but scientists have come up with some possible explanations and theories.

5. Challenge your students to come up with their own explanations of how the solar system formed. Let them discuss these in small groups for about 3–5 minutes, or until you sense that interest is about to wane. Tell them that they may illustrate their ideas on paper, if they find it helpful.

From a Swirling Cloud

1. Tell your students that they will use water and pepper as a model for the formation of the solar system. The pepper will represent the material from which the solar system formed. The water will represent empty space.

2. Pass out the containers of water and the stir sticks, one for each team. Next visit each team and put two good shakes of pepper into each container. Tell the students that you are putting a thin scattering of "gas and dust" into their containers of "empty space."

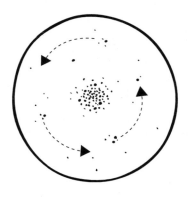

Note: If you have enough pepper shakers to go around, you may have students add their own pepper. They will be repeating the activity, and if they have their own shakers they may choose to add more pepper to model and watch the formation of a heavier star. Be alert to any behavior that might cause pepper to get into someone's eyes.

3. Tell them that gravity pulls the gas and dust together into a swirling mass. Have a student in each team give three or four quick counterclockwise stirs to the water,

then stop stirring and observe what happens. Let them know that they will soon repeat the activity, so that eventually everyone in the team will get a chance to stir.

4. Have students discuss what they see in their teams, and then call on students to describe how the system of water and pepper evolves. [They should note that most of the pepper gravitates toward the middle and forms a large clump. Some of the pepper grains do not join the clump, but swirl around at various distances from the center.]

5. Ask your students how they think this might represent the formation of the planets. If they do not mention it themselves, tell them that the clump in the center represents the Sun, and the pieces orbiting it represent the planets. Tell them that in this model other forces actually drew the pepper grains together in the center, but that in the real solar system it was gravity.

6. The students can easily disturb the system with their stir sticks and form the pepper into a disorderly cloud again. Give them a few minutes to form, un-form and re-form their solar systems several times. Encourage them to report any new observations they may make.

Going Further

Consider passing out the "Your Galactic Address" sheet to students. If you are presenting this outside of te United States, substitute a map of the appropriate country.

For your information, the solar system is at approximately this location in the Milky Way Galaxy.

What pulls the pepper to the middle?

When a real planetary system is formed, gravity pulls the matter together. In this activity the pepper simply follows the currents of water. At the very bottom of the container there is a slight current toward the middle. The pepper that sinks to the very bottom forms the clump, while the pepper that stays suspended higher up simply orbits the center. The reason for the flow toward the center at the bottom is complex and students definitely do not need to know it in order to appreciate the formation of an orderly system out of a chaotic cloud.

YOUR GALACTIC ADDRESS

Name: _____

Your seat
Draw your classroom, and mark an "X" where you sit

Name: _____

Your classroom
Draw your school, and mark an "X" where your classroom is located.

School: _____

Your City and State
Mark an "X" where your city is located, on this map of the USA.

City and State: _____

Your Country
Mark an "X" where your country is located, on this map of the Earth.

Country: _____

Your Planet
Mark an "X" where your planet is located, on this map of the solar system.

Planet: _____

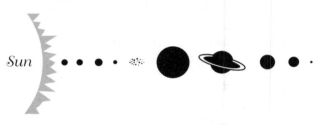

Your Planetary System
The solar system is about ⅔ of the way from the center to the edge of the galaxy. It is on the outer edge of the "major spiral arm." Mark an "X" where your solar system is, on this map of the Milky Way Galaxy.

Planetary System and Galaxy: _____

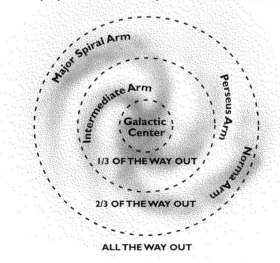

Session 2: The Solar System—Travel Brochures

Overview

In this session, teams of students are assigned an object in the solar system. They begin work on stations for a solar system "tour," which takes place during Session 3 of this activity. The stations include travel brochures and a model which will also be used during Session 4 of this activity. The size of the model planet is assigned so that all of the planets and other solar system objects are to the same scale. Students may complain that it is too small, but you can assure them that there is a good reason for that which they will discover later in the unit.

Your students will need time in addition to this session to work on their stations. You may want to give them class time to work on them, assign them as homework, or a combination of the two. Some teachers have found that the quality of work on the travel brochures is higher if the students work on it as homework rather than during class. The stations must be completed before you will be able to do Sessions 3 or 4.

We have provided information sheets on the Sun, Luna (the Earth's Moon), all the planets, two moons of Jupiter, a moon of Saturn, the asteroid belt, and the Oort comet cloud. You could add information on other moons of Jupiter, such as Callisto or Ganymede, which is the largest moon in the solar system. The GEMS guide Moons of Jupiter has information on all of Jupiter's moons.

In addition to the fact sheets at the end of this session (pages 61–76), more information can be found on The Nine Planets web site at http:// www.seds.org/billa/tnp/nineplanets.html or The Nine Planets for Kids web site at http://www.tcsn.net/afiner

What You Need

For the class:

❑ clay

❑ scissors, tape, and glue

❑ markers and/or colored pencils

❑ construction paper

❑ 1 copy of the Solar System Stations Sign-Up sheet (master on page 58)

❑ several copies of each of the fact sheets (masters on pages 61–76) for your own reference

❑ *(optional)* sample travel brochures from a local travel agency

For each team of 2–4 students:

❑ 1 large, black garbage bag

❑ 1 copy of the Solar System Tour Station sheet (master on page 59)

❑ 2–4 copies of the fact sheet for the astronomical body upon which the team is working

For each student:

❏ 1 Solar System Travel Brochure sheet (master on page 60)

Getting Ready

1. Make one copy of the Solar System Stations Sign-Up (master on page 58) for the class to use when choosing their station.

2. Make copies of the Solar System Tour Station (master on page 59) for the teams to use while designing their station.

3. Make one copy of the Solar System Travel Brochure (master on page 60) for each student to use for creating their own travel brochure.

4. Make several copies of the fact sheets (masters on pages 61–76). Keep several complete sets for your own reference and have enough extra to distribute one copy of the astronomical body they've selected to each student on a team.

5. Have the craft material together in an easily accessible location.

Introducing the Tour

Many students are surprised that we haven't traveled to Mars. Tell them that in the solar system tour they will get an idea of how far away the planets are, and perhaps will then understand why there haven't been human astronauts sent on missions to any of the planets.

1. Ask your students to imagine how "cool" it would be if they could take a tour of the solar system and travel to the different planets to check them out. Ask them if they have heard of any explorations of other planets by spacecraft. Tell them that every planet except Pluto has been investigated by spacecraft. These spacecraft have carried cameras, and other scientific instruments, but no humans. The only extraterrestrial site explored by *human astronauts* is our Moon.

2. Let your students know that they will get to tour the solar system and "check out" all the planets within the classroom, and that they will create the tour themselves. Tell them that they will be divided into teams, and that each team will be assigned to some part of the solar system.

3. Explain that they should focus on what it would be like to be in their assigned part of the solar system. They

should examine questions such as whether their planet (or moon or comet or asteroid) is in the Sun's lifezone. What pleasures and hardships would a lifeform have to endure in their part of the solar system? What type of suit or other adjustments would humans need?

4. Let students know that how much fun the tour is depends on them. Tell them that if a team makes a boring picture, and just copies down some number facts, it won't be that interesting. Challenge each team to put energy into making the stations interesting and fun, so that the tour will be fun for the whole class.

5. Distribute the Solar System Tour Station student sheet, one for each team. Go through the assignments. When you come to the model-making assignment, tell them that they will get a fact sheet that has the proper diameter for their model. Review the concept of *diameter* if necessary. Tell them that some teams may be surprised when they see what the diameter of their model is supposed to be. Tell them that there is a good reason for this which they will see later. (If any team wants to make a different-sized model, they may do so as a substitute for the drawing, **but they must also make a model of the assigned size.**)

Describing the Travel Brochure Assignment

1. Tell your students that each of them will be responsible for writing up a travel brochure for their part of the solar system. Pass out the Solar System Travel Brochure sheet, one to each student. Encourage them to be creative, and to say things in a fun way—not simply listing facts and measurements.

2. As an example of how to include accurate facts in a humorous manner, as opposed to simply listing them, read the following two examples aloud:

> A list of facts:
>
> **The Atacama Desert**
> - There are places in the Atacama desert where rainfall has never been recorded.
> - Atacama has many cloud-free days.
> - The Atacama is in the southern hemisphere, where the seasons are opposite those of the northern hemisphere.

- The population is 202,259 in a region of 29,000 square miles.

Facts presented in a more interesting manner:

Visit the Atacama desert!

- Do you have athletes foot or other fungi on your body? Then come to Atacama. It's so dry in some parts, rainfall has never been recorded! Those fungi will dry up and wither away.

- Do you love sunny days? Do cloudy days get you down? Come to Atacama where it's almost always sunny! It's also great for star gazing on the many cloud-free nights!

- Tired of cold Decembers? Come to Atacama, where December is summer, and one of our hottest months of the year.

- Tired of crowds? Come to Atacama, where there is an average of only 7 people per square mile.

3. If you've collected sample travel brochures from your local travel agency, show them to students.

4. Encourage students to use poems, illustrations, models, comparisons, and/or describe strange activities (such as jumping when there's less gravity) that could be performed at their chosen location. Remind them that although the descriptions and format may be playful, the factual information should be accurate.

5. Draw an example on the board of what the layout of each station will look like, including title, drawing, size-model, and travel brochures. Suggest that they may choose to place or tape small size-models on a sheet of paper, so they won't get lost.

6. Show students where the garbage bags and craft materials (clay, construction paper, scissors, tape, glue, etc.) will be located. To avoid chaos and congestion, you may want to have one "runner" from each group in charge of getting materials.

7. Assign the teams to their planetary stations, or let them choose, using the Solar System Stations Sign-Up sheet. Depending on the size of your class, you may or may not choose to include Saturn's moon, Titan, and Jupiter's moons, Europa and Io, in the tour.

To avoid the passing on of misinformation in the travel brochures, you may want to have the students turn in a rough draft that you can review before they make a final draft.

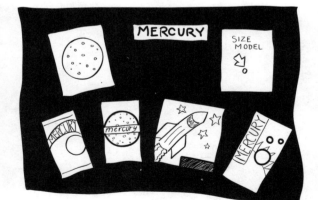

8. Some stations involve more information than others, so you may want to assign them to appropriate teams. If you have a smaller class, but would like to include the afore-mentioned moons, then you will need to have some students work alone.

9. After teams have selected an astronomical body to work on, distribute the appropriate fact sheet to the team—one for each student. Review with the class the format of the information on the fact sheets, if necessary. Brainstorm other resources students can use, and see the "Resources" section on page 135.

Many teachers recommend the Nine Planets web site: http://www.seds.org/billa/tnp/nineplanets.html. Also helpful is the Nine Planets for Kids web site: http://www.tcsn.net/afiner

You may want to post a number of helpful web sites on the board as students begin their research work. See page 155 for more suggestions. Students will no doubt discover much on their own.

SOLAR SYSTEM STATIONS SIGN-UP

STATION	NAME(S)
Sun (Sol)	
Mercury	
Venus	
Earth (Terra)	
Luna (Earth's Moon)	
Mars	
Asteroid Belt	
Jupiter	
Europa (one of Jupiter's moons)	
Io (one of Jupiter's moons)	
Saturn	
Titan (one of Saturn's moons)	
Uranus	
Neptune	
Pluto	
The Oort Cloud 9 (cold distant comets)	

SOLAR SYSTEM TOUR STATION

Include these at your station:

❑ **Title** —Write out the name of your planet, moon, Sun, comet cloud, or asteroid belt.

❑ **Drawing**—Draw a color picture of it.

❑ **Model**—Make a "size model" (or scale model) of it. Use clay, a ball, marble, papier mâché, wadded-up newspaper, or whatever seems appropriate. Small planets can be done with clay, but larger planets will need to be a ball or wadded up paper. It does not need to look like what you've chosen, but it must be the right size.

❑ **Travel brochures**—One from each member of your group.

You may store your materials in your group's garbage bag. On tour day, your group will use the garbage bag as the "space" background for your station on a table.

SOLAR SYSTEM TRAVEL BROCHURE

Your Assigned Part of the Solar System: _____

Your Name: _____

Due: _____

Use this checklist to make sure you have included:

- ❑ You must include at least 5 pieces of accurate and interesting information about your planet/moon/Sun/asteroid/comet in your text. Use this information in a fun way to make everyone want to vacation there.

- ❑ You should also include what the surface is like, temperature, atmospheric gases, gravity, and energy sources (such as the Sun or volcanoes).

- ❑ At least 1 drawing of your planet/asteroid/comet/Sun/moon.

- ❑ Describe what it looks, smells, and feels like there. This should be based on real information!

- ❑ In addition to the information sheet provided, you should have at least two other sources. List them on the back of your brochure.

- ❑ Make your brochure exciting, colorful, neat, interesting, and factual. Be creative, funny, artistic, poetic—go where no person has gone before!

Write out the interesting information in your own words.

DON'T COPY. DON'T WRITE DOWN THINGS YOU DON'T UNDERSTAND.

Some ideas you might want to use and/or ideas to launch your own inspiration:

- Make a drawing of what an unprotected person might look like if they landed there.

- Describe what people should wear there.

- Describe any special activities a person could do there.

- Write a short poem about it.

- Make up a nickname for it, or use one you've heard.

- Make true or false question flip cards with the answers underneath.

- Write a song or rap about it by changing the words of a song or rap you know. Write out the words, or record it for people to listen to on a "walkman."

Sun

Diameter: about 865,000 miles
Mass: 333,000 x Earth's mass
Surface gravity: 28 times the Earth's gravity
Time for one rotation: about 26 Earth days

The Sun is the star closest to Earth. Its volume is 1.3 million times that of Earth and it contains over 99% of all the mass of the solar system. One hundred and nine Earths could fit across its diameter. The Sun is about 70% hydrogen and 28% helium.

Life of the Sun: The Sun is a yellow star formed from a cloud of gas and dust over 4.5 billion years ago. It is thought to have formed as part of a cluster of other stars which have separated, so now the Sun is alone. Yellow stars last about 10 billion years, and our star is nearly 5 billion years old, so you could call it middle-aged. The Sun shines by turning its hydrogen fuel into helium. Every second, 600 million tons of hydrogen are converted. When the Sun runs out of hydrogen fuel, it will turn into a red giant star as it starts using its helium as fuel. At that point, it will emit 1,000 times as much light as now, and will be 100 times larger, big enough to engulf Mercury and Venus. It will then shrink to a white dwarf, about the size of the Earth. After billions more years it will cool down and end its life as a cold dark "black dwarf."

Inside the Sun: The core of the Sun is 27,000,000°F. The pressure at the core is about 340 billion times Earth's air pressure at sea level. The intense heat and pressure cause nuclear reactions to take place. The energy generated in the core of the Sun takes about 1 million years to reach the surface.

The Surface of the Sun: The surface of the Sun is made up of swirling gases called the photosphere. It has a temperature of 11,000°F. Sometimes huge flame-like clouds explode from the photosphere. Short bursts are called solar flares. Huge "prominences" up to 100,000 miles high may last for months. The dark patches of cooler gases are called sunspots. Surrounding the photosphere is an unseen layer of gas called the chromosphere. Above the chromosphere is a layer of gas called the corona, which means "crown." The Sun gives off a flow of gas and energetic charged particles called the solar wind, which streams through the solar system at over 200 miles per second.

Exploration: *Never look directly at the Sun, because it may cause blindness.* Solar astronomers use special telescopes that cut down the light. In the 1980s the Ulysses probe was launched to study the Sun from space. This probe gave the first views of the Sun from its north and south poles. For more recent information, check out the web site of the Solar and Heliospheric Observatory, a joint European and U.S. Mission to learn more about the Sun at http://sohowww.nascom.nasa.gov/

Mercury

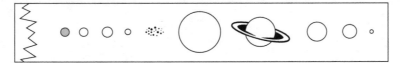

Diameter: 3000 miles
Average distance from the Sun: 36 million miles
Mass: about $\frac{1}{20}$ of Earth's mass
Surface gravity: about $\frac{1}{3}$ of Earth's gravity
Length of day (the time it takes to turn around once): 59 Earth days
Length of year (the time it takes to orbit the Sun): 88 Earth days
Atmosphere: almost none
Moons: none

The closer a planet is to the Sun, the faster it orbits. As the planet closest to the Sun, Mercury clips along at 30 miles per second. In Roman mythology Mercury was the messenger of the gods, and the planet got its name because it orbits the Sun faster than any other planet. Mercury is hard to see from Earth because of the Sun's glare.

Temperature: Since Mercury is so close to the Sun, it gets almost 10 times as much heat, light, and radiation per square foot as Earth. During the day, surface temperatures can reach 800°F. Because it has so little atmosphere, it can't hold the heat at night, so it gets freezing cold—hundreds of degrees below zero. Of all the planets in the solar system, Mercury has the biggest changes in temperature from day to night.

Atmosphere: Mercury captures small amounts of solar wind gases (mostly helium) that stream by from the Sun. These gases never remain very long in the atmosphere because the gravity of Mercury is weak, and the daytime temperature gets very high. The atmosphere is only one million-billionth the density of Earth's atmosphere. Sound cannot travel without air, so Mercury is a silent world. Mercury is one of the most inhospitable planets around the Sun, because the surface is continually bombarded by unfiltered sunlight, which includes dangerous ultraviolet radiation and X-rays.

Geology: Mercury is one of the rocky, or terrestrial, planets in the solar system. Because it has a weak magnetic field and high density, scientists think Mercury has a large iron core. Above the core is the mantle, a layer of compressed molten rocks. On top of the mantle is a solid, rocky crust.

Mercury's surface has many craters caused by asteroids and comets smashing into it, like the Earth's Moon. Unlike the Moon, Mercury has only one lava plain—the 800 mile diameter Caloris Basin. The largest crater is called Beethoven, and is 400 miles (625 kilometers) across. Mercury may have volcanic activity beneath the surface which causes "hot" regions on opposite sides of the planet. There is also evidence of ice in the protected shadows of craters near the north pole.

Exploration: Mariner 10 mapped part of Mercury in 1974 and 1975, but because it always flew by the same side, there is more to be explored.

Venus

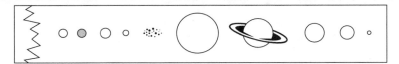

Diameter: 7500 miles

Average distance from the Sun: 67 million miles

Mass: about $^{19}/_{20}$ of Earth's mass

Surface gravity: about $^9/_{10}$ of Earth's gravity

Length of day (the time it takes to turn around once): 243 Earth days

Length of year (the time it takes to orbit the Sun): 225 Earth days

Atmosphere: mostly carbon dioxide, thick

Moons: none

The second planet from the Sun, Venus is named after the goddess of love and beauty in Roman mythology. Venus comes closer to the Earth in its orbit than any other planet. Other than the Sun and the Moon, it is the brightest object in the sky. Venus is often called the morning star or the evening star, because it looks like a bright white star and can be seen near the horizon in the morning or early evening. Thick clouds make it impossible to see the surface of Venus through telescopes. Before it was examined by space probes, many thought it might be Earthlike, with oceans, swamps, and maybe even life.

Temperature: Venus' thick carbon dioxide atmosphere acts like a greenhouse, and keeps heat from the Sun from escaping, making it more than 900°F! That's more than hot enough to melt lead. Scientists have studied Venus to predict what may happen to Earth as we add more carbon dioxide and other gases by polluting our own atmosphere, and increase the greenhouse effect on Earth.

Atmosphere: Venus' atmosphere is 96% carbon dioxide that is so thick and heavy that the atmospheric pressure is more than 90 times Earth's, enough to crush a person in seconds. Venus has sulfuric acid clouds. It is always raining sulfuric acid, but the rain never reaches the surface. It vaporizes and forms clouds again high in the atmosphere. Because of the cloud cover, the stars and our Sun can't be seen from the surface.

Geology: Venus is a rocky, or terrestrial, planet that is similar to the Earth in size, weight, and composition. It has been called Earth's sister planet. Like Earth, Venus has a dense iron-nickel core which is probably partly liquid, a mantle of molten rock on top of that, and an outer crust. Venus may have large active volcanoes.

Exploration: Venus was first studied by Galileo, who noticed that it has phases like the Moon. It has been explored by many spacecraft since the 1960s. These include the Soviet Union's Venera 1 in 1961 to Venera 16 in 1983, and Vega 1 and 2 in 1984. Because it is such a harsh environment, the landers from these missions transmitted data for only 2 hours at the most before breaking down. The United States has sent Mariners 2, 5, and 10, 2 Pioneers in 1978 and Magellan in 1990, which mapped the surface with radar that could scan right through the clouds.

Earth (Terra)

Diameter: 8000 miles

Average distance from the Sun: 93 million miles

Length of day (the time it takes to turn around once): 1 Earth day

Length of year (the time it takes to orbit the Sun): 365 Earth days

Atmosphere: mostly nitrogen (78.08%) with plenty of oxygen (20.95%), some water vapor (0%–3%), and a trace (0.03%) of carbon dioxide

Moons: one (Luna)

Earth, the third planet from the Sun, is the only body of the solar system that we know for certain has life. Human beings are one among many millions of Earth's diverse lifeforms—on land and in both fresh and salt water. Most life on Earth depends on the Sun's energy. Plants use the Sun's energy to make food, and other lifeforms get their energy either from eating plants or by eating other animals that get their energy from eating plants. It has recently been discovered that some lifeforms get their energy from volcanic heat and chemicals deep in the oceans. The Earth's molten nickel-iron core and the planet's daily rotation creates a large magnetic field. Along with the atmosphere, this magnetic field protects us from almost all the harmful radiation from the Sun.

Temperature: The Earth's atmosphere acts like a blanket around the Earth and helps keep heat from the Sun from escaping. This is called the greenhouse effect. Without this effect the Earth would be much colder.

Atmosphere: Earth has enough gravity to hold onto an atmosphere, which is rich in life-giving oxygen. Earth's atmosphere was once mostly carbon dioxide, but long ago blue-green algae, one of Earth's early lifeforms, made oxygen from carbon dioxide through photosynthesis. The Earth's atmosphere protects us by burning up most meteors before they can hit the planet. High in the atmosphere, a form of oxygen called ozone screens out some of the dangerous radiation from the Sun.

Weather on Earth is caused by the Sun heating up the air. The air moves from hot areas toward cold areas, making wind. The Sun's heat causes liquid water to evaporate into water vapor, which cools, turns into liquid or solid, and falls to Earth as rain, snow, or hail. This water cycle is one of the keys to life as we know it.

Geology: Earth is one of the rocky, or terrestrial, planets in the solar system. Radioactive materials in the Earth keep its insides very hot. Rising hot material under the Earth's crust causes large slabs of crust to shift. This causes earthquakes and volcanoes, and helps give the Earth's surface its shape. Wind and water erosion also change the shape of Earth's landforms.

Exploration: Earth has been explored more fully than any other planet, yet many mysteries remain. The deep ocean has undiscovered lifeforms. Beneath rocks and ice lie clues to our planet's past that may help us discover its future. Satellites and space ships give us views of the Earth that show how oceans, deserts, forests, grasslands, and cities all interact with and affect each other, helping us visualize and seek global solutions to pressing environmental issues.

Luna (Earth's Moon)

Diameter: 2000 miles

Average distance from the Earth: about $^1/_4$ million miles

Mass: about 1% of Earth's mass

Surface gravity: about $^1/_6$ of Earth's gravity

Length of day (the time it takes to turn around once): about a month

Time it takes to orbit the Earth: about a month

Atmosphere: none

All the planets in the solar system have moons, except Mercury and Venus, but Earth's Moon is one of the biggest. Our Moon is named Luna, but most people just call it "the Moon." It is a good object for beginning astronomers to study because the features on its surface can be seen with the naked eye. It does not shine with its own light, but instead reflects sunlight. Luna is thought to have formed about 4 1/2 billion years ago, possibly from leftover debris from a crash of a Mars-sized object into the young Earth. Other astronomers think it may have broken off from the Earth. Another possibility is that it was a rock captured by Earth's gravity, or that it formed from dust and rocks around the young Earth.

The Moon's gravity is one-sixth that of the Earth's which means that a person who weighs 180 pounds on Earth weighs only 30 pounds on the Moon. The sky is always black, because there is no atmosphere. Earth looks colorful and beautiful from the Moon.

Temperature: Because it has no atmosphere to hold in heat, the Moon's temperature changes a lot. It can range from −275°F at night to 280°F during the day.

Atmosphere: The Moon has no atmosphere because it doesn't have enough gravity to hold one. Since sound needs air to travel, there is no sound on the Moon!

Geology: The Moon has two main types of terrain that can be seen with the naked eye. The lighter areas are mountainous and heavily cratered, and the darker areas are flat plains called "maria," caused by ancient lava flows. Since the Moon doesn't have an atmosphere to protect it against comets, asteroids, and meteors, it is covered with craters from bombardments throughout its history. The intense early bombardments smashed, melted, buried, or mixed a lot of the original Moon rocks.

Because there is no weathering of rocks without an atmosphere or water, the Moon has unweathered rocks more than 4 billion years old. The Moon is considered geologically dead, but there still are occasional large impacts. It has a small iron and sulfur core, surrounded by a layer of partially melted rock. The crust is a relatively thick layer of solid rock.

Exploration: Apollo missions explored the Moon in the 1960s and 1970s. On July 20, 1969, Neil Armstrong became the first person to walk on the Moon. Eleven more astronauts have "Moon-walked" since then, and the Moon is still the only body in the solar system, other than Earth, that people have visited. Information from the Lunar Prospector mission in 1998 suggests that there might be ice buried in some of the deep craters near the Moon's poles where the Sun never shines.

Mars

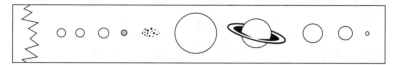

Diameter: 4000 miles
Average distance from the Sun: 142 million miles
Mass: about $^1/10$ of Earth's mass
Surface gravity: about $^1/3$ of Earth's gravity
Length of day (the time it takes to turn around once): 25 Earth hours
Length of year (the time it takes to orbit the Sun): 687 Earth days
Atmosphere: thin carbon dioxide
Moons: two small moons (less than 20 miles across)

The fourth planet from the Sun, Mars is often called the red planet. From Earth, it looks like a bright red star. Mars is covered with iron rocks—so the red is just rust. Because of its fiery color, the planet was named after the Roman god of war. Many people have imagined Mars as a likely location for extraterrestrial lifeforms—books and movies about "Martians" abound. Astronomers looking through telescopes 100 years ago even thought they saw canals built by Martians. None of the missions to Mars have turned up any evidence of life.

Many astronomers believe that the combination of ultraviolet radiation from the Sun, extreme dryness, and the rusting of the soil prevent living things from forming. We know that there probably once was flowing water on Mars, because of the dry river channels that have been found. There is very little water vapor in the atmosphere now, but there are large amounts of ice below the surface.

Mars has two tiny moons, Phobos and Deimos. They may have been asteroids that came near and were captured by Mars' gravity. Deimos is the smallest known moon of a planet in the solar system and orbits around Mars in seven hours! It moves so fast that if you were on Mars you would see it rise in the west and set in the east—several times a day! The orbit of Phobos is decaying, and it is predicted it will collide with Mars within the next 30 million years.

Temperature: Mars has two icy poles like Earth. During the winter the poles have frozen carbon dioxide (dry ice) which makes them look brighter, but in the Spring they shrink. Mars has a maximum temperature of 75°F and a minimum of −190°F.

Atmosphere: Mars has an atmosphere much thinner than Earth's, made up of 95% carbon dioxide. Winds of 45 to 90 meters per second can whip up a lot of very fine red dust. The dust is so fine, it stays in the air for months. These make the sky look pink. Although the Martian atmosphere only has ~1/1000 as much water as the atmosphere on Earth, this is enough to form some clouds, frost, and fog.

Geology: Mars is one of the rocky, or terrestrial, planets in the solar system. It has the largest known mountain in the solar system, a volcano called Olympus Mons, which is about three times as tall as Mount Everest. A series of canyons called Valles Marineris is ten times longer and four times deeper than the Grand Canyon. Mars has a core of iron, smaller than the cores of other rocky or terrestrial planets. Its mantle is made of silicate materials (like sand), with a crust of iron-rich rusty rocks.

Exploration: Mars has been explored by orbiting space craft Mariner 4 in 1965 and Mariner 9 in 1971. Viking 1 and 2 both landed on Mars. The Pathfinder landed in 1997. Its six-wheeled rover studied the material in the rocks. NASA plans to launch additional missions to Mars about every two years.

Asteroid Belt

Actual Size: from specks of dust to pieces
a few hundred miles across; the diameter of Ceres (the
largest asteroid) is 580 miles

Distance from Sun of main asteroid belt: about 200 to 325 million miles

Atmosphere: none

Asteroids are chunks of irregularly shaped rock and metal, ranging in size from specks of dust to pieces hundreds of miles across. Many are potato-shaped. There are millions of asteroids in the solar system, but most of them are in what is called the asteroid belt, between Mars and Jupiter. They are made of the same material that formed the planets. Many astronomers think that they were not able to clump together to form a planet because the gravity of nearby Jupiter kept them apart.

Although most asteroids are in the asteroid belt, there are other families of asteroids in other parts of the solar system. There is a group of asteroids in the same orbit as Jupiter called the Trojans, some orbiting in front of it, and some behind. Another group, the Apollo family, crosses the path of Earth. Sometimes asteroids crash into planets. One of the most well known theories about why the dinosaurs and other prehistoric animals became extinct is that an asteroid crashed into Earth making a giant explosion and sending up enough dust to block out a lot of sunlight for a long time.

Another asteroid belt has been discovered inside Mercury's orbit, and still another past Pluto called the Kuiper Belt. Some astronomers think that Pluto is not a planet, but just a large asteroid from this belt.

Temperature: Those asteroids that orbit far from the Sun are very cold and covered with ice, but those that orbit closer are warmer, and mainly made of rock.

Atmosphere: Asteroids are small, and do not have enough gravity to hold onto atmospheres.

Geology: Asteroids are all made up of different minerals and chemicals. Some are rocky while others are rich in metal. Some have organic, carbon materials, and many have water trapped in them.

Exploration: A planet between Mars and Jupiter was mathematically predicted in the 1700s. After 16 years of searching for this mystery planet, the largest asteroid, Ceres, was discovered by accident in 1801. Since then, about 10,000 asteroids have been cataloged. In 1997, for example, an object 300 miles in diameter that orbits the Sun far beyond Pluto was found, and given the catchy name, 1996TL66. Its elliptical orbit ranges from 3.2 billion miles from the Sun to 14 billion miles. A few good photographs of asteroids have been taken by space probes on their way to other planets. For instance, Dactyl—a moon of the asteroid Ida—was photographed by the Galileo Probe on its way to Jupiter. Many astronomers would like to systematically search for all the asteroids that might come near to Earth, but this has never been done.

Jupiter

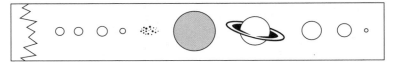

Diameter: about 89,000 miles

Average distance from the Sun: 484 million miles

Mass: 318 times Earth's mass

Surface gravity: about 2 $\frac{1}{2}$ times Earth's gravity

Length of day (the time it takes to turn around once): 10 Earth hours

Length of year (the time it takes to orbit the Sun): 12 Earth years

Atmosphere: thick and cloudy

Moons: four large ones, and at least 12 smaller ones

Jupiter, named after the king of the gods in ancient Roman mythology, is the fifth planet from the Sun, and by far the largest. Over 1300 Earths could fit inside Jupiter, and it has more matter than all the other planets put together. Of the four gas giants, it is the closest to the Sun. Jupiter has an extremely intense magnetic field—thousands of times more powerful than Earth's.

Jupiter's four largest moons can be seen through small telescopes and even binoculars. Along with its many moons, a comet is occasionally caught in orbit around Jupiter. In 1994 a shattered comet, Shoemaker-Levy 9, struck Jupiter causing enormous explosions that left marks in the cloud patterns which lasted for nearly a year.

Temperature: The shrinking of Jupiter's core together with radioactive decay of elements in the core releases heat. Jupiter actually gives off more heat itself than it gets from the Sun! The core of Jupiter is an intense 50,000°F, but the upper clouds are freezing at −220°F.

Atmosphere: Jupiter's atmosphere is mostly made of hydrogen and helium (with tiny amounts of methane and ammonia), and is thousands of miles deep. This huge planet spins so rapidly (a day is 10 hours) that it causes strong winds and giant storms. The Great Red Spot is a giant hurricane that has lasted for more than 340 years! Lightning bolts have been observed in Jupiter's cloud tops.

Geology: Although Jupiter is huge, it has a small rocky core, surrounded by a vast ocean of hydrogen in liquid and metallic form. Above this is an enormous atmosphere. Rather than being able to "land," a probe would sink for a long time into this deep atmosphere. Jupiter is considered a "Jovian" planet, one that is mostly atmosphere, as opposed to a "terrestrial" planet, which is mostly rock.

Exploration: In 1610 Galileo discovered four of Jupiter's moons: Io, Europa, Ganymede, and Callisto. His discovery made an important contribution toward making the case that the Earth was **not** the center of the Universe. The Voyager 1 and 2 spacecraft took photos of the outer cloud layers of Jupiter in 1979. Voyager also revealed that Jupiter has rings that can't be seen from Earth, made of dust about the size of smoke particles. In 1996 the Galileo mission reached Jupiter. It sent a probe into the clouds to measure the conditions there. After hours of successful study, this probe was crushed deep in the thick atmosphere. The main Galileo orbiter has continued to photograph Jupiter and its moons.

Europa (one of Jupiter's moons)

Diameter: 2000 miles
Average distance from Jupiter: 400,000 miles
Mass: 1% of Earth's mass
Surface gravity: about $^1/_7$ of Earth's gravity
Time it takes to orbit Jupiter: 3.6 Earth days
Atmosphere: a trace of oxygen

Europa (yur-ROH-pah) was named after one of Jupiter's mortal lovers in ancient Roman mythology, who became Queen of Crete. A little smaller than Earth's Moon, in photographs from a distance, Europa has the smoothest surface in the solar system—it looks as smooth as a cue ball, without mountains, valleys, or major craters. Some think it looks like a cracked eggshell, because it has what look like veins across its surface. The surface appears to be criss-crossed by dark lines. They may be cracks, but they aren't very deep, and no one knows for certain what they are. Many astronomers suspect that Europa has giant ice plates that float and move around like icebergs.

Europa is tugged at by the gravity of Jupiter, the largest planet in the solar system. The tidal pull of Jupiter heats up Europa's insides as it is squeezed back and forth. Astronomers do not know if there is enough heat to melt the ice on Europa. Ice flow patterns and ridges on Europa suggest there may be melted or slushy water beneath the hard ice surface. There is even a possibility of ice-spewing volcanoes and geysers.

Temperature: Colder than −200°F at the surface, but probably much warmer inside.

Atmosphere: Europa has a very thin atmosphere of oxygen. The oxygen is not released by plants, as on Earth. Instead, sunshine breaks down the water molecules in the ice creating hydrogen and oxygen gas. The hydrogen gas is light, and escapes into space, but Europa's gravity holds onto the heavier oxygen for a while, before it escapes. Although the atmosphere reaches about 125 miles above Europa's surface, it is so thin that if it was at the surface pressure of Earth, it would all fit in about 12 Houston Astrodomes! The air pressure is about one-hundredth of one-billionth of the air pressure at the surface of the Earth.

Geology: Europa probably has a solid (rocky) core, but the surface seems to be a three-mile thick crust of water ice. Beneath the ice, models show that Europa may have oceans of liquid water as deep as 30 miles or more—possibly even more water than all the oceans of Earth!

Exploration: Voyagers 1 and 2 photographed Europa in 1979. The Galileo mission has made amazing new discoveries about Europa during its orbit of Jupiter.

Io (one of Jupiter's moons)

Diameter:	2000 miles
Average distance from Jupiter:	260,000 miles
Mass:	about $1/60$ of Earth's mass
Surface gravity:	about $1/6$ of Earth's gravity
Time it takes to orbit Jupiter:	1.8 Earth days
Atmosphere:	thin sulfurous gases

In ancient Roman mythology, Io was another of Jupiter's lovers, who, as the legend goes, was turned into a white cow by Jupiter to protect her from Hera, the queen of the gods. She also became the cow goddess queen of Egypt. The moon Io is a little larger than Earth's Moon and is sometimes called the "pizza" moon, because in some photos it resembles a pizza, with its volcanoes looking like toppings!

Io is one of the most interesting moons in the solar system. It is not only tugged at by the gravity of Jupiter, the largest planet in the solar system, but also by the gravity of Europa and Ganymede, two other large moons of Jupiter that are nearby. This tug-of-war makes for tidal bulging on Io as high as 330 feet, and makes Io the most volcanically active body in the solar system. When these gravitational forces squeeze it back and forth like a rubber ball, Io's insides heat up. The hot insides are released in huge volcanic explosions that can reach 200 miles above the surface. Although it is less than a third the size of Earth, Io gives off twice as much heat!

Io is swept by Jupiter's magnetic field, which strips away about one ton of material per second. As this material passes through the magnetic field, it also generates more electrical energy than all the power stations in the United States generate! Io may be the only moon in the solar system with a strong magnetic field of its own.

Temperature: Because it is far from the Sun it can be −230°F. Where sulfur has been heated in volcanic eruptions the temperature can be 600°F or more. There is a large hot spot that may be a sulfurous lava lake, although the estimated 60°F temperature there is not hot enough for the lava to be molten.

Atmosphere: Io has an extremely thin atmosphere of sulfur dioxide, sodium, potassium, and magnesium (and perhaps other gases) that come from volcanic activity. They remain in the atmosphere only a while, and then are pulled away toward Jupiter.

Geology: Io is mostly made of molten rocky material but it may have an iron-rich solid core. The surface is mostly sulfur, which is white when cold, and orange and red when melted by volcanic activity.

Exploration: The Voyager fly-by photographed Io in 1979, counting 200 volcanoes, nine of them erupting at the time! These were the first volcanic eruptions seen anywhere in the solar system other than on Earth. The Galileo mission has made more discoveries.

Saturn

Diameter: 75,000 miles

Average distance from the Sun: 890 million miles

Mass: 95 times Earth's mass

Surface gravity: slightly greater than Earth's gravity

Length of day (the time it takes to turn around once): 10 $\frac{1}{2}$ Earth hours

Length of year (the time it takes to orbit the Sun): 29 $\frac{1}{2}$ Earth years

Atmosphere: thick and cloudy

Moons: six large ones, and at least 12 smaller ones

Saturn was named after the son of Uranus (the sky) and Gaia (the Earth), in ancient Greek mythology. The sixth planet from the Sun, Saturn is a gas giant, and the second largest planet in the solar system. Jupiter, Neptune, and Uranus all have rings, but Saturn has by far the most spectacular!

The rings are made of countless pieces of icy rock, some as small as dust and some as big as houses. Scientists estimate that there are ten thousand rings! Some think that the rings are leftover debris that failed to gather to form a moon. Others think they are the remains of a moon that was torn apart by Saturn's gravity, or that crashed into another moon. Saturn has 18 moons that have been discovered, more than any other planet in the solar system, and there may be more.

Temperature: Saturn gives off more heat than it receives from the Sun. That means it is probably still warm from the time it was formed and has not finished cooling off. Still the average cloud temperature is a bracing −290°F to −300°F.

Atmosphere: The atmosphere is mostly hydrogen and helium, with small amounts of methane. Winds over 1,100 mph can blow in Saturnian storms, but near the poles the winds stop.

Geology: Although Saturn has 95 times more mass than Earth, its average density is less than water. That means that if there was an ocean of water big enough, Saturn could float in it. Because it has such low density and it spins so fast (1 day is about 10 and one-half hours), Saturn has a "tummy" bulge at its equator. Saturn has a core composed of silicates and minerals, surrounded by metallic hydrogen. It has an outer layer made up of hydrogen and helium, which is gas towards the surface, but liquid towards the center.

Exploration: In 1610, Galileo was confused by Saturn's rings, partly because his telescope did not show them clearly. He thought they might be a triple planet. In 1655 Christian Huygens, a Dutch astronomer, more clearly observed and described the rings. But it was not until 1856 that James Clerk Maxwell explained that the gravitational field would tear any solid ring to pieces, and concluded that they must be composed of numerous small particles in orbit around the planet. Voyager 1 and Voyager 2 photographed Saturn in the early 1980s. In 1997 the Cassini space probe was launched toward Saturn. It will take seven years to get there.

© 1999 by The Regents of the University of California, LHS-GEMS. *Messages form Space.* **May be duplicated for classroom use.**

Titan (one of Saturn's moons)

Diameter: 3200 miles
Average distance from Saturn: 760,000 miles
Mass: about $1/40$ of Earth's mass
Surface gravity: about $1/7$ of Earth's gravity
Time it takes to orbit Saturn: 16 Earth days
Atmosphere: cloudy atmosphere with pressure $1 \frac{1}{2}$ times the air pressure at the surface of Earth

In ancient Greek mythology, the Titans were one of the sets of offspring of Uranus (the Sky) and Gaia (the Earth). Titan (TY-tun) is Saturn's largest moon, and the second largest in the solar system, after Ganymede, one of Jupiter's moons. Although Titan is a moon, it is bigger than the *planets* Mercury and Pluto! It is unusual for a moon to have an atmosphere, but Titan's atmosphere is more dense than the atmospheres of Mercury, Earth, Mars, and Pluto.

Other than Earth, Titan is the only body in the solar system that may have oceans and rain—not water rain, but ethane and methane rain, which on Earth are flammable and odorless ingredients of natural gas. Scientists think there may be ethane-methane lakes on Titan as well as other complex organic materials. Such organic materials can be building blocks of life, and some aspects of the chemical composition of Titan are thought to be similar to what may have existed on Earth before life began. On the other hand, Titan is much colder than Earth, has no water, and its atmospheric and other conditions differ from Earth in many important ways.

Temperature: Colder than −290°F.

Atmosphere: Titan is the only moon in the solar system with a heavy atmosphere. Its atmosphere is 90% nitrogen, which is also mixed in with methane and ethane (which would be poisonous to animals on Earth). The Sun breaks down the methane, which makes hydrocarbons like the smog over cities on Earth. The thick smog hides the surface, and makes it difficult to study.

Geology: Astronomers know that Titan has at least some solid surface, but most of this moon has remained hidden by its thick orange "smog" clouds.

Exploration: Voyager I flew by Titan in 1980, but could not see into the thick clouds. In 2004 the Cassini spacecraft is scheduled to visit Titan, and plans call for a probe to be dropped into its atmosphere.

Uranus

Diameter: 32,000 miles

Average distance from the Sun: 1,800 million miles

Mass: about 15 times the Earth's mass

Surface gravity: about $^9/_{10}$ of Earth's gravity

Length of day (the time it takes to turn around once): 18 Earth hours

Length of year (the time it takes to orbit the Sun): 84 Earth years

Atmosphere: thick and cloudy

Moons: at least 17

Uranus (the Sky) was the first ruler of the universe in ancient Greek mythology, and, with Gaia (the Earth), had many offspring, among them the Titans. The planet Uranus is a cold gas giant with 17 moons and at least 11 thin black rings around it. The rings are made up of ice boulders and fine dust. Uranus is twice as far from the Sun as Saturn, and although all the planets from Mercury to Saturn had been discovered long before, Uranus was not discovered until 1781. Uranus is not easily visible to the naked eye; Neptune and Pluto are never visible to the naked eye.

One of the strangest things about Uranus is that its axis is tilted far more than any other planet. Other planets spin around a vertical axis, but Uranus spins much more horizontally, as if it were on its side. Astronomers think it may have been tilted as a result of a collision or collisions with another large body or large chunks of material early in its history.

The moons of Uranus are all battered looking, with many craters, cliffs, and rough terrain. The largest five moons are Miranda, Ariel, Umbriel, Titania, and Oberon. Miranda, the closest of the larger moons to Uranus, has two unusual rectangular surface features that look as if they had been smoothed by the flat side of a huge knife. Some astronomers have speculated that Miranda may also have been affected by the collision that tilted the axis of Uranus—the moon may have been shattered into pieces which then clumped back together.

Temperature: Uranus' outer layers never get warmer than about −300°F, but at its core it may be 11,000°F or more.

Atmosphere: Uranus's atmosphere is 72% hydrogen, 26% helium and 2% methane (or natural gas). Methane in the upper atmosphere reflects blue and green light, giving Uranus its blue-green color. Uranus has winds that blow at speeds up to 360 mph.

Geology: Uranus has a rocky core a little larger than the planet Earth. Thousands of miles above the core is a thick region (mantle) of water, ammonia, and methane so cold that it is mostly in ice and liquid form. The outer layer is composed of hydrogen and helium gases.

Exploration: Uranus was discovered in 1781 by William Herschel. In 1986 Voyager 2 photographed Uranus, but could not see beneath the haze of the upper atmosphere. Voyager 2 also made the first detailed photographs of the rings and surfaces of the moons of Uranus.

© 1999 by The Regents of the University of California, LHS-GEMS. Messages form Space. **May be duplicated for classroom use.**

Neptune

Diameter: 31,000 miles
Average distance from the Sun: 2,800 million miles
Mass: 17 times the Earth's mass
Surface gravity: slightly more than Earth's gravity
Length of day (the time it takes to turn around once): 19 Earth hours
Length of year (the time it takes to orbit the Sun): 165 Earth years
Atmosphere: thick and cloudy (similar to Uranus)
Moons: two big ones and at least six smaller ones

Named after the Roman mythological god of the sea, Neptune is the gas giant farthest from the Sun. It is so big that about 60 Earths could fit inside it. Like the other gas giants, Neptune also has a ring system. There are three rings, one of which is somewhat dim. The rings are made up of particles of rock and ice, some of which are a few kilometers across, and some the size of dust. The larger ones are sometimes called "moonlets." The rings may be leftover debris from comets or asteroids that smashed into Neptune's moons.

Neptune has at least eight moons. Its largest moon, Triton, has wrinkled features that have not as yet been explained. It may also have icy volcanoes.

Temperature: The average cloud temperature is −365°F.

Atmosphere: The winds of Neptune blow at speeds of up to 1,200 miles per hour—stronger than on any other planet! The atmosphere is made up of hydrogen, helium, and methane. The methane reflects green and blue light, and gives Neptune its bluish color, similar to Uranus. Neptune has a huge dark storm that rotates around the planet, called the Great Dark Spot. It is so big that the Earth could fit in it! There are white clouds of methane crystals high above the bluish atmosphere. Voyager photographed one of these clouds "scooting" around Neptune, about every 16 hours. This cloud has been called "the scooter."

Geology: Neptune has a small rocky core, which is surrounded by an ocean of liquid water, ammonia, and methane (what we call natural gas).

Exploration: Neptune's existence and position were mathematically predicted in the 19th century by astronomers in England and France, based on irregularities in the orbit of Uranus. It was first actually observed and identified in 1846 by Johann Galle and a German astronomy student, less than one degree from its predicted position. The two larger moons of Neptune were discovered by astronomers with telescopes. Voyager discovered six more moons of Neptune when it flew by in 1989!

© 1999 by The Regents of the University of California, LHS-GEMS. Messages form Space. **May be duplicated for classroom use.**

Pluto

Diameter: 1,500 miles

Average distance from the Sun: 3,680 million miles

Mass: about $^1/400$ of Earth's mass

Surface gravity: about $^1/25$ of Earth's gravity

Length of day (the time it takes to turn around once): 6 Earth days

Length of year (the time it takes to orbit the Sun): 248 Earth years

Atmosphere: thin, if any

Moons: one

Pluto, named for the Greek and Roman mythological god of the underworld, was discovered in 1930—the last planet found in our solar system. It is extremely difficult to observe from Earth because it is so distant and so small. Pluto is almost forty times farther from the Sun than Earth. It is so far that it is very dark, and, from Pluto, the Sun would only look like a very bright star.

Pluto is a very strange planet. It is a small rocky planet in a part of the solar system where all the other planets are gas giants. All other planets in the solar system have orbits that are fairly circular, but Pluto's is not. Its oval-shaped orbit sometimes brings it closer to the Sun than Neptune. Pluto was closest to the Sun in 1989, and remained closer than Neptune until March 14, 1999.

Pluto has one moon, Charon, named after the mythological boatman who operated the ferry across the river Styx to Pluto's underworld realm. Charon is about half the size of Pluto. Many astronomers wonder whether Pluto should really be classified as a planet. It could be considered a large asteroid.

Temperature: Extremely cold; −370°F to −390°F.

Atmosphere: Pluto may have a thin methane atmosphere when it is closest to the Sun. As it moves away from the Sun the methane freezes and falls to the surface. The frozen methane turns a reddish color in sunlight. Ices of water and ammonia are also present.

Geology: Pluto has a rocky core surrounded by a layer of water ice. Its surface is frozen methane (natural gas). Charon seems to be covered with water ice, not methane ice.

Exploration: Even after Neptune was discovered, astronomers continued to observe irregularities in the orbits of Uranus and Neptune itself. In 1905, Percival Lowell and William Pickering calculated the position of another planet, which might account for these irregularities by its gravitational pull. Astronomers began searching, but it was 25 years before a young astronomer, Clyde Tombaugh, photographed Pluto about 5 degrees from the predicted position. Interestingly, Pluto's gravitational attraction is too small by itself to account for the disturbance in the orbits of Neptune and Uranus, and some astronomers think there may be another undiscovered planet in the solar system. Pluto is the only planet that has never been explored by a space probe. Beyond Pluto lies the recently discovered Edgeworth-Kuiper Disk of "ice dwarfs" or minor planets. NASA is developing a robotic reconnaissance mission to Pluto-Charon using lightweight advanced-technology hardware components and advanced software technology. The Pluto mission plan calls for launch when this technology is ready around 2010 or later.

The Oort Cloud (cold distant comets)

For your model: Use chalk dust.

Diameter: various sizes; the solid core or nucleus of Comet Halley was about 10 miles across; no other has been observed

Distance from the Sun: out to 6 trillion miles

Time it takes to orbit the Sun: from a few years, to many millions of years

Atmosphere: none (for most objects)

Although the comet cloud has never been seen, many astronomers believe it exists far beyond Pluto. It is thought to be made up of the leftovers from the cloud that formed the solar system, and it contains billions of chunks of ice and dust called comets. Once in a while, when one falls toward the Sun, it becomes visible to us. A few have settled into orbits that bring them back near the Sun on a regular oval path. Most of the rest remain in the depths of space far beyond Pluto.

When a comet is far from the Sun it is a large chunk of dirty ice, but as it gets closer to the Sun its surface ice turns to vapor (it sublimates), forming a head of gas called a coma. The coma may be a million miles wide, but the original ball of ice and dust—the nucleus of the comet—is very rarely over 100 miles wide!

The Sun's radiation sweeps the coma and dust into two tails, one tail of gas and one tail of dust. Usually, the dust tail is yellow, and the gas tail is bluish. The tail always points away from the Sun, so, as the comet moves away from the Sun, it travels tail first. A hydrogen envelope that is not visible from Earth also forms, as hydrogen is chemically released. As it travels near the Sun, the comet loses material. It is estimated that Halley's Comet will completely decay after about 2,300 more trips around the Sun.

Many astronomers think that some asteroids are comets that have lost almost all their ice and gases. Gas and dust left by a comet is littered along its orbit. Every August, the Earth passes through the orbit of a comet named Swift-Tuttle. The dust burns up in the atmosphere as a shower of meteors also known as shooting stars. Meteorites are any lumps of interplanetary rock big enough to survive Earth's atmosphere without burning up, so they actually hit the Earth. Most are the size of a fist, but some are larger. One large meteor crashed in Arizona 25,000–40,000 years ago, making a crater almost a mile across!

Ingredients: The nucleus of a comet is made up of ice (hydrogen and oxygen) and solid grains (carbon, nitrogen, iron, potassium, calcium, manganese, and silicon).

Some Recent Comets: Kohoutek (1974), Halley's (1986), Hyakutake (1996), Hale-Bopp (1997).

Exploration: In 1986, Halley's Comet was studied by a number of space probes. The Giotto probe photographed the comet from about 300 miles away, giving the first view of the nucleus of a comet. NASA's Mission Stardust has been sent out to collect material from the tail of a comet. To learn more about it, check out http://stardust.jpl.nasa.gov/

© 1999 by The Regents of the University of California, LHS-GEMS. Messages form Space. **May be duplicated for classroom use.**

Session 3: Touring the Solar System

Overview

In this session, the students tour the solar system model made by the class. After reviewing the questions and format of the data sheet, the students rotate through each of the stations in teams, recording information at each location. After completing the tour, they fill in their responses to the questions on their data sheet, and are given the opportunity to return to the stations for further research. The teacher then leads a discussion of the question, "Where in the solar system besides Earth might life exist?"

What You Need

For each team of 2–4 students:
- ❐ completed assignments from Session 2 of this activity

For each student:
- ❐ 1 double-sided copy of the Tour of the Solar System data sheet (masters on pages 79–80)

Getting Ready

1. Plan where each team will set up its station. Be sure to consider the flow of student "traffic."

2. Make a double-sided copy of the Tour of the Solar System data sheet (masters on pages 79–80) for each student.

Preparing the Tour

1. Remind your students that the message from space at the beginning of the unit seemed to depict the planets in the star system where the message originated. Let them know that although they can't see these distant planets, they can study the planets within their own solar system to use as a model—a way to envision what some of the aspects of the distant planetary system might be.

2. Review some of the main things that scientists think a planet needs in order to be suitable for life, such as: proper temperature, liquid water, a star with a long lifespan, etc. Ask students if they want to add any other ideas to the list.

3. Have your students set up their stations at designated locations around the room. Start with the Sun, then position the others in order around the classroom: Sun, Mercury, Venus, Earth, Mars, Asteroid Belt, Jupiter, Saturn, Uranus, Neptune, Pluto, and the Comet Cloud. Also display any moons, if you've chosen to include them.

4. Distribute the Tour of the Solar System data sheets to each student. With the whole class, read aloud the questions. Tell your students that these questions are to be answered **after completing the tour,** but they should be thinking about them during the tour.

5. Show students the Chart of Key Life Factors on the other side of the Tour of the Solar System data sheet, and explain that they should record information about the planets on this chart **during the tour,** to help them respond to the seven questions after the tour. Review how each category relates to conditions considered suitable or necessary for life.

Beginning the Tour

1. Have the teams stand or sit at the station they designed. Tell them the direction in which they are to move on to the next station when you announce that it is time to switch. Allow at least two minutes per station.

2. When all the groups have finished and returned to their original stations, tell them to use the information they've collected to respond to the seven questions on the Tour of the Solar System sheet. Let them know that they may revisit any of the stations while working on the questions.

3. When everyone has completed the questions, you may want to share and discuss their responses with the whole class, or discuss the more general question, "Using the information you've gathered, where in our solar system besides Earth do you think there might be life?"

Names: _____

TOUR OF THE SOLAR SYSTEM

1. Which planet would be the best for a record-breaking high jump contest? Why?

2. Where do you think it's *most* likely for us to find life in our solar system other than Earth? Why?

3. Where do you think it's *least* likely for us to find life in our solar system other than Earth? Why?

4. What planet or moon do you think is the best candidate for Earthlings to build settlements on? Why?

5. What planet or moon do you think is the worst candidate for Earthlings to build settlements on? Why?

6. Which is the "coolest" looking planet?

7. Which is the weirdest looking planet or moon?

TOUR OF THE SOLAR SYSTEM
CHART OF KEY LIFE FACTORS

	Surface: Is it a rocky surface like Earth's, or is it a gaseous surface?	Liquid Water: Is it too cold or too hot for liquid water?	Gravity: Is there enough gravity to hold on to an atmosphere?	Atmosphere: Is there an atmosphere? If so, what kind of gases are in it?	Source of Energy: Is there energy available from sunlight or from volcanoes?
Sun					
Mercury					
Venus					
Earth					
Luna (Earth's Moon)					
Mars					
Asteroid Belt					
Jupiter					
Europa (one of Jupiter's moons)					
Io (one of Jupiter's moons)					
Saturn					
Titan (one of Saturn's moons)					
Uranus					
Neptune					
Pluto					
Comet Cloud					

Session 4: Putting the Planets in Their Places

Overview

The teacher leads students through an activity that demonstrates the vast distances in the solar system. A few students carry their "size models" of the planets outdoors to previously marked positions representing their planet's distance from the Sun in the classroom. The distances of the remaining planets from the Sun in the model are illustrated using a local map and a world map. Through this demonstration, students get a visual representation of how much of space is empty, and the vast distances between planets and stars.

Students usually wonder why the models they made in the previous sessions had to be so small. As they see how far apart the planets are they should see the reason. If students are still not satisfied with the smallness of the models you may have them make a larger scale model as described in the Going Further section at the end of this activity.

What You Need

For the class:

❒ the size-model of a solar system object that students made in Session 2 of this activity

❒ local map (Internet sites such as **maps.yahoo.com** will create a map centered around your school's address)

❒ globe or world map

❒ *(optional)* a commercial non-scale model of the solar system

❒ *(optional)* surveyor's flags or other easily carried, highly visible markers

Getting Ready

1. Determine the locations that you will use for the planets in the scale model. The Sun will be in your classroom. The chart that follows tells how far each planet should be from the Sun.

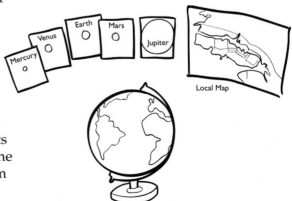

Local Map

2. For the nearer planets, Mercury, Venus, and Earth, (and possibly Mars) estimate or pace out the distance from your classroom, and locate some landmark at about the proper distance. For example, you will be able to describe the location of the planet as "by the corner of the fence near the driveway," or "by the forked tree near the playing field."

3. For the more distant planets and other objects, use a local map. Using the scale on the map, find a location that is about the correct distance from your school, using local landmarks familiar to your students. You might have a planet be "at the library downtown," or "at the fast food restaurant on Highway 24."

4. List all the planet and other space object locations on the chart so that you will be able to locate them with your students in the schoolyard and on the map. In this scale, you will need to use a globe to show students the distances to the Oort Comet Cloud and Alpha Centauri, the nearest star.

POSITION OF MODEL PLANETS FOR THE SCALE MODEL OF THE SOLAR SYSTEM

In this model, 46 inches = 1 million miles

Name	Model size	Model distance from the Sun metric	English	Your model	Actual distance from Sun miles	AU
Sun	1 m	0	0	your classroom	0 miles	0 AU
Mercury	3.5 mm	42 m	138 ft.		36 million miles	.4 AU
Venus	9 mm	78 m	257 ft.		67 million miles	.7 AU
Earth	9.5 mm	109 m	357 ft. .07 mile		93 million miles	1 AU
Luna	2.5 mm	about the same as Earth		11 inches from Earth	about the same as Earth	
Mars	5 mm	166 m	544 ft. .1 mile		142 million miles	1.5 AU
Asteroid Belt	chaulk dust	230-380 m	.15-.25 mile		200-325 million miles	2.2-3.5 AU
Jupiter	10 cm	566 m	.35 mile		484 million miles	5.2 AU
Europa	2 mm	about the same as Jupiter		19 inches from Jupiter	about the same as Jupiter	
Io	2.5 mm	about the same as Jupiter		12 inches from Jupiter	about the same as Jupiter	
Saturn	9 cm	1 km	.65 mile		888 million miles	9.6 AU
Titan	3.5 mm	about the same as Saturn		1 yard from Saturn	about the same as Saturn	
Uranus	3.5 cm	2.1 km	1.3 miles		1,790 million miles	19.2 AU
Neptune	3.5 cm	3.3 km	2 miles		2,800 million miles	30.1 AU
Pluto	2 mm	4.3 km	2.7 miles		3,680 million miles	39.5 AU
Comet Cloud	chaulk dust	as far away as 7,000 km	4,300 miles	about $\frac{1}{6}$ of the way around the Earth	as far away as 6 trillion miles over 60,000 AU/1 light year	
Nearest Star System (Alpha Centauri)	1 m	30,000 km 18,630 miles		about $\frac{3}{4}$ of the way around the Earth	26 trillion miles over 275,000 AU about 4.4 light years	

AU = Astronomical Unit (or distance from Earth to Sun, 93 million miles)

Please note: *Many of the numbers in this chart have been rounded off in order to make them more accessible to students and align as well as possible with activities in the guide. In addition, there are differences, usually slight, in the facts and figures given by leading astronomical sources and organizations. We have tried our best to walk that line as well. We hope you and your students find this chart useful. A number of excellent additional sources for information are listed in the "Resources" section of this guide.*

Distances in Space

If you have a commercial solar system model you may want to introduce the session with it. First, show students the solar system model. Ask them what they think the model is meant to show. [Most of these models show what the Sun and planets look like, and the relative distances from the planets to the Sun.] Explain that some companies that make this kind of model adjust the sizes of the planets. They make the smaller ones too big so they will be more interesting to look at, and they make the Sun too small so it will fit in the package and to be more convenient to display. Explain that such store-bought models can give the wrong idea of what a planetary system is like. Tell students that the class will use the small models they made to show what a true scale model of the solar system is like.

If you have maps of the same area that have a different scale, you may want to show and discuss them with the class.

1. Have your students sit with their team at the station they created. Draw their attention to the size-model of the Sun, and point out that in this model, the Sun is 1 meter in diameter.

2. Tell each team to hold up their model, and ask them to notice the size of the planets relative to the Sun at this scale. Point out some of the large and small planets, and how much smaller they are than the Sun.

3. Ask the members of the Earth team to walk around the room, and hold their model up against the other objects in the solar system. Remind them that when we're on it, the Earth seems huge to us—about 25,000 miles in circumference and 8,000 miles in diameter—but it appears very small when compared to some of the other objects, such as Jupiter (about 89,000 miles in diameter).

4. Tell students that in a scale model all the objects and distances are reduced by the same proportion. If they had wanted to make bigger planet models, what would that mean about the size of the Sun model and the distances between objects? [They would have to be bigger too.]

5. Explain that in a scale model, not only the **sizes** of the objects should be to scale, but the **distances between** the objects should also be to scale. Within the scale of a 1 meter Sun and a 1 centimeter Earth, the class will now be able to see how much space the model solar system occupies.

6. Hold the Earth next to Mercury and ask the class to compare their diameters. (Mercury is less than half the diameter of Earth.) Tell students to keep this idea of the scale of Earth's diameter in mind throughout the activity as they also consider the distances between the planets.

7. Ask students where in the room Mercury might belong. Let them know that it will be outside of the room entirely! Lead the class outside or, if you have a window, send the Mercury team outside with their model as the rest of the class watches. Direct the Mercury team to the location you've designated (see "Getting Ready"). If you have surveyor's flags or other markers have the Mercury team mark their location.

8. Ask your students to imagine how many Earth diameters (about 8,000 miles) it would take to span the distance from the Sun to Mercury. [About 4,500 Earths lined up side by side would reach from the center of the Sun to Mercury!]

9. Point out that using Earth-diameters may be one way to compare sizes of things in the solar system, but it is an awkward way to compare the extremely large distances between things. Astronomers use the average distance from the Sun to the Earth as a standard measure. This is called an *Astronomical Unit,* or AU for short. Mercury is about four-tenths of an AU from the Sun.

10. Direct the Venus team to its designated location. Next have the class guess where Earth will be, and then direct the Earth team to the position you've designated. **This latter distance represents one AU in the model.** Continue the procedure with the Moon. Also do Mars, if space allows. If you're using them, have the teams take and place the surveyor's flags or other markers.

11. Point out to your students that, by far, the main ingredient of the solar system is empty space. You may want to emphasize this more than once.

12. Ask the Asteroid Belt team how practical they think it would be to take their asteroid model to its typical place, 300 meters (about a quarter of a mile) away. Ask the same question of the Saturn team, whose model goes one kilometer (more than half a mile) away! If you're outside with the class, return to the classroom.

Plotting on a Map

1. Use the local map to mark the locations of all the planets and other space objects that are too distant to fit in your schoolyard. See if students know any landmarks in the places on the map where you are indicating the positions. Be sure to point out the following:

> **Earth**—is 11,625 "Earths" from the Sun, which equals one AU.

> **Mars**—Discuss why people have never been to Mars. It may be one of the closest planets, but it's still very far away.

A one way trip carrying humans to Mars would take many months. Exactly how long depends on the available technology. Since the astronauts would have to wait to return until Mars and Earth are both on the same side of the Sun again, they'd have to stay on Mars 1.5 years. That suggests at least a three year mission—and three years worth of heavy provisions.

Pluto—Hold up Pluto. Ask students to imagine that the tiny model is in an orbit almost three miles from the classroom. Ask, "Can you see why it's hard for us to see Pluto from our planet?" It's *so* far (almost one-half million "Earths" from the Sun—or about 40 AUs) and so small!

2. Remind your students that the planets are not fixed in one location in space as shown in diagrams, but orbit around the Sun at that distance from the Sun. (Most of the planets orbit in a near-circular ellipse; Pluto's orbit is more elliptical.) Encourage students to imagine the tiny planets in the model orbiting around the classroom Sun.

3. Ask your students if they have any ideas where the nearest star system, Alpha Centauri, would be located in this model. Tell them that it would be about 3/4 the distance around the Earth. Show a spot on the globe about three quarters of the way around the Earth from your school's location.

4. Tell your students that spaceships can currently travel at about 25,000 mph (the circumference of the Earth per hour). Point out to your students that traveling at 25,000 miles per hour, it would take about 120,000 years to get to Alpha Centauri, and that's the *closest* star system. Let them know that this is the main reason SETI scientists believe it is so unlikely that extraterrestrials could come to Earth—the distances are truly enormous!!

Rather than telling your students the information in Step 4, you could have them mathematically compute it by taking the 26 trillion mile distance to the Alpha Centauri system, dividing it by 25,000 (mph) and figuring out how many years that would be!

Our nearest star (aside from the Sun) is actually a system of three stars called the Alpha Centauri system. It includes Proxima Centauri and Alpha Centauri A and B. They are over 4.3 light years away. Proxima Centauri is a dim red dwarf star, Alpha Centauri A is a yellow star like our Sun, and Alpha Centauri B is a white star. The Alpha Centauri system is located in the constellation Centaurus, which unfortunately is not visible in much of the Northern Hemisphere.

Going Further

Designing Other Models

Your students can design models of the solar system at other scales, either larger or smaller than the one described in this activity. The Exploratorium science center in San Francisco has a site on the Internet that can assist you and your students (**www.exploratorium.edu/ronh/ solar_system/**). You enter the size you would like for the Sun and the computer delivers a table that shows the proper sizes and distances for your model. Students who are familiar with computer spreadsheets could also design this kind of application for themselves.

Smaller Model:

Have students design a scale model of the solar system (out to Pluto) that would fit entirely in your schoolyard. They will have to measure the space they have available and use that to determine the proper scale for their model. Then they will have to use the scale to calculate the proper sizes and positions of the solar system objects.

Larger Model:

Tell students that some museums and planetaria have created much larger scale models of the solar system. The Community Solar System at the Lakeshore Museum in Peoria, Illinois is listed as the largest by the 1997 Guiness Book of World Records. The model is centered around a Sun 11 meters in diameter. Pluto is a one inch sphere in a furniture store 40 miles away! More information about this model and other information about the solar system can be found on the Internet at **www.bradley.edu/las/phy/ solar_system.html**

Students can choose a scale that would make a solar system model fit any setting they like. They do not have to actually build it, but they can plot possible positions for the Sun and planets on a map.

Activity 4: Dear Extraterrestrials...

Overview

In Activity 3, students studied the solar system, its formation, its contents, and its size. This activity gives students the chance to communicate what they know about the solar system in messages to outer space lifeforms. The messages are in the form of pictures to be sent in reply to those who sent the message to Earth in Activity 1. Instead of beaming their pictures into space with radio telescopes, students exchange them with each other and attempt to interpret each other's messages.

See page 159, "Assessment Suggestions," for a number of assessment opportunities for the entire unit.

For the teacher, this activity can serve as an assessment of what the students have learned about the solar system and which facts about the solar system students consider most important.

What You Need

For the class:

- ❐ the overhead transparencies of the seven-page Message from Space from Activity 1, Session 2
- ❐ 1 overhead transparency of each of the Arecibo, Pioneer, and Voyager messages (masters on pages 93–95; see the note about the Pioneer message in the "Getting Ready" section)
- ❐ an overhead projector

For each student or team of 2–4 students:

- ❐ 2 pieces of paper
- ❐ pencils or other drawing material
- ❐ *(optional)* graph paper

Getting Ready

1. Have on hand the seven transparencies of the Message from Space from Activity 1, Session 2. Make one transparency of each of the Arecibo, Pioneer, and Voyager messages (masters on pages 93–95). The Pioneer message includes drawings of an unclothed man and woman. If you wish, you could tape a piece of paper over (or white-out) the mid-sections of the two people. Make sure that most of the outline of the spacecraft shows in the background.

2. Have a piece of paper ready to keep the key to the Arecibo message covered until after the students have had a chance to interpret it for themselves.

Reviewing the Message from Space

1. Tell your students that they are going to design a message to send back to the extraterrestrials who sent the message from space that they interpreted earlier in the unit. Ask students what information they think would be important to send. You may want to mention any of the following if your students do not:

- how our solar system formed

- what planets and other objects are in our solar system

- different types of stars, and what type of star we have

- distances between the planets and the Sun

- Earth's history: geologic, biological, and/or political, cultural

- types of planets

- information about moons, asteroid belts, and the comet cloud

2. Quickly review the Message from Space from Activity 1, Session 2 on the overhead projector. Find out what further ideas students have come up with about the message since the last time the class discussed it. Ask your students what information seems to have been important to those who sent the message.

3. Note that to communicate any information about "how big" or "how many" would seem to require some form of basic mathematics for counting and measurement. Examine the message once more to see if those who sent it might have tried to communicate a measuring system or a numbering system. [There is a numbering system at the top of page 1 of the message. It is used in various ways throughout the message. It is not necessary that you and your students recognize and decode all of its meanings. Stu-

dents may recognize that, at the top of page 7 of the message, the numbers are used to count the planets in our solar system, and also on page 7 there is an attempt to depict the distance from the Earth to the Sun, the Astronomical Unit or AU, as a standard of measurement.]

Looking at Examples

1. Show your students the Arecibo message on the overhead projector. Keep the part with the explanation of the message covered. Explain that this message was designed by a SETI scientist named Frank Drake and broadcast into space as a binary signal, a stream of bits that formed the pieces of the picture.

2. Challenge students to interpret the Arecibo message. Remind them that this is not a message *from* space, but a message from Earth that attempts to convey scientific information about ourselves, our planet, and solar system.

3. Gradually uncover the key to the Arecibo SETI message and explain each section. Ask the class if there is any part they think should not have been included, or that could be improved. Ask, "How might distant lifeforms interpret the picture of a person and the radio telescope if they didn't know what the real ones look like?" Remind students that this particular message had to be very short to fit on a grid of limited size.

4. Next show students the transparency of the plaque that was attached to the Pioneer space probes. (If you haven't covered it, be prepared for the predictable reaction.) Tell them that this message was not a binary coded radio message, but a picture that was attached to a pair of space probes that have now left the solar system. Some time, perhaps millions of years from now, some extraterrestrials may find it!

5. Encourage a short discussion of the meaning of the Pioneer message. Ask students if they would have shown the people with or without clothes. If they would show the people wearing clothes, what kind of clothes would they choose?

6. Show students the Voyager transparency. Explain that on the Voyager space probes there was a "Sounds of Earth" recording, with a picture showing how to build a device to

Students may wonder how ETs could be expected to figure out what size the grid should be. The Arecibo message contained 1,679 bits. The number 1679 is the product of two prime numbers, 23 and 73. There are only two ways to make a grid, one wrong guess and one right guess. We assume that if distant lifeforms received a message from space they would be just as interested in it as we would be, so they would work on interpreting the message until they succeeded.

NASA has a web site that can play selections from "Sounds of Earth." Reach it directly through NASA (http://vraptor.jpl.nasa.gov/voyager/record.html) or by following links from www.lhs.berkeley.edu/gems

play it. Ask students what sounds from Earth they would choose for extraterrestrials. Briefly show them the list of sounds included on the recording.

Making the Message

1. Have students work individually, or in teams of two to four. Pass out two pieces of paper and drawing materials. Before they begin, let them know that when finished, other members of the class will attempt to interpret their messages, so they should be somewhat secretive as they work.

2. Have students/groups list on one piece of paper the things that they would want to communicate to an extraterrestrial civilization. Tell them that a message with a lot of information may be interesting, but a simple message will be easier to understand. Have them circle the items they plan to include in their message.

3. Have students draw their picture-message twice. One drawing should be on the paper with the list of things they are trying to communicate. They may add more writing on the page to help explain the meaning of the picture. On the other piece of paper they should copy just the drawing—without any written explanation. This is the page that shows the message that the ETs will actually see.

4. If you'd like, have students turn their pictures into binary messages on graph paper. They should choose a rectangular grid that will fit the picture and fill in the squares to create the message.

5. Have teams of students exchange messages. If students created the message individually, have them work in pairs to interpret the messages so they can discuss their ideas with their partner.

6. Reconvene the entire class and have a team of students show the message that they "received" and explain how they interpreted it. See if other students have ideas about what the message means. The student(s) who created the message should not comment at this time. Later they can be given the opportunity to tell what they really meant. Continue discussing messages as time allows.

ARECIBO MESSAGE

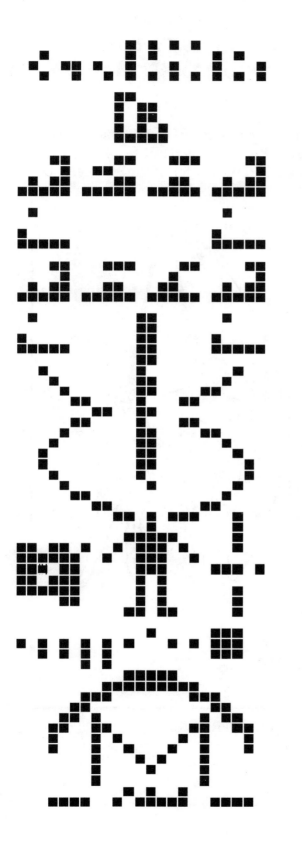

A binary system of counting showing one to ten from right to left.

A list of some of the most important organic compounds that make up living things on Earth. The structure of these materials is described mathematically using the numbering system shown above to list the element in the compounds.

A picture of the arrangement of compounds to form a DNA molecule. This molecule is in every known living thing. Aliens might be familiar with molecules like it.

A picture of the twisted spiral of a DNA molecule.

In the center is a picture of a person. On the left is the human population of the Earth. On the right is a measurement of the height of a person.

A picture of our Sun and nine planets. The third planet, Earth, is shown slightly closer to the picture of a person.

A picture of a radio telescope. Anyone who receives this message will probably have one like it. The pattern at the bottom is meant to show how wide the dish of the Arecibo radio telescope is.

This pictorial message was engraved on gold plaques on the Pioneer 10 and Pioneer 11 spacecraft. The Pioneer spacecraft were launched in 1972 and 1973.

A hydrogen molecule. The wavelength of the radio emissions of hydrogen (21 cm) is used as a universal distance measurement in this picture.

A map that shows the position of the Solar System. We are in the middle, and the lines reach out to 14 pulsars. The longest line reaches to the center of the galaxy.

Two human beings standing in front of a Pioneer spacecraft.

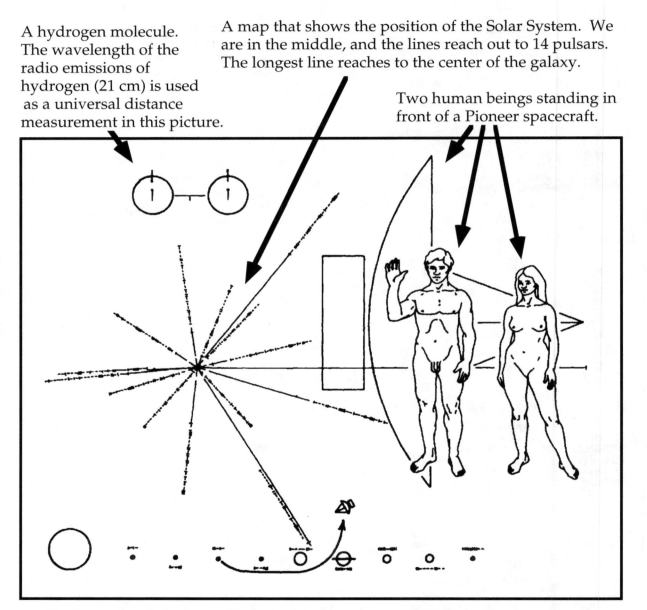

The Sun and the nine planets. The path of the Pioneer spacecraft is shown.

A recording called "Sounds of Earth" was included on a 12-inch copper disc on Voyager 1 and 2, which were launched in 1977. The disc includes some pictures and sounds from Earth, along with instructions and materials for making a record player.

Selections from "Sounds of Earth"

Greetings spoken in 55 different languages, ancient and modern.

Sumerian, Arabic, Urdu, Italian, Ila (Zambia), Akkadian, Romanian, Hindi, Nguni, Nyanja, Hittite, French, Vietnamese, Sotho, Swedish, Hebrew, Burmese, Sinhalese, Wu, Ukranian, Aramaic, Spanish, Greek, Korean, Persian, English, Indonesian, Latin, Armenian, Serbian, Portuguese, Kechua, Japanese, Polish, Luganda, Cantonese, Dutch, Punjabi, Nepali, Amoy (Min dialect), Russian, German, Turkish, Mandarin, Chinese, Marathi, Thai, Bengali, Welsh, Gujarati, Kannada, Telugu, Oriya, Hungarian, Czech, Rajasthani.

An hour and a half of music from many times and places.

Bach, Brandenburg Concerto No. 2 in F,
Java, court gamelan, "Kinds of Flowers,"
Senegal, percussion,
Zaire, Pygmy girls' initiation song,
Australia, Aborigine songs,
Mexico, Mariachi band,
Chuck Berry, "Johnny B. Goode,"
New Guinea, men's house song,
Japan, shakuhachi flute music,
Bach, "Gavotte en rondeaux" for violin,
Mozart, "The Magic Flute, Queen of the Night" aria,
Georgian S.S.R., chorus, "Tchakrulo,"
Peru, panpipes and drum,
Louis Armstrong, "Melancholy Blues,"
Azerbaijan S.S.R., bagpipes,
Stravinsky, "Rite of Spring, Sacrificial Dance,"
Bach, "Prelude and Fugue in C, No. 1,"
Beethoven, "Fifth Symphony, First Movement,"
Bulgaria, song, "Izlel je Delyo Hagdutin,"
Navajo Indians, "Night Chant,"
Holborne, Paueans, Galliards, Almains and Other Short Aeirs,
Solomon Islands, panpipes,
Peru, wedding song,
China, ch'in, "Flowing Streams,"
India, raga, "Jaat Kahan Ho,"
Blind Willie Johnson, "Dark Was the Night,"
Beethoven, "String Quartet No. 13 in B flat."

Other Sounds, Natural and Human-Made

volcanoes, earthquake, thunder, mud pots, wind, rain, surf, crickets, frogs, birds, hyena, elephant, chimpanzee, wild dog, footsteps, heartbeat, laughter, fire, speech, the first tools, tame dog, herding sheep, blacksmith, sawing, tractor, riveter, Morse code, ships, horse and cart, train, tractor, bus, auto, F-111 fly-by, Saturn 5 lift-off, kiss, mother and child, life signs, pulsar

Activity 5: Making a Planetary System

Overview

In this session, the students apply information they've learned about the solar system in previous activities to design a planetary system where life could have developed, based on the message from space at the start of the unit. The models are drawn on a large piece of paper and include one of a variety of star types. Students are asked to make their models realistic, but are also encouraged to be creative and imaginative. The planetary system they design will be the setting for a science fiction story they write at the end of the unit.

As a guideline for their models, the students use information that they interpreted from the message. They also apply what they've learned about star types and lifezones. Students also need to take into account an additional requirement for a planet that supports life—a rocky surface. The distinction between rocky Earth-like planets and gas giant planets is readily apparent from the previous activities, but in this activity it is more explicitly stated.

A special feature on "The Drake Equation," which focuses on the probability of life existing elsewhere, is included as a "Going Further" at the end of this activity. We highly recommend it as one of the best ways to convey an important "message" of this unit. On the one hand, as students have learned, distances in space are enormous, so there is thought to be a minuscule likelihood of lifeforms actually visiting us (sensationalistic films and tabloids notwithstanding). On the other hand, given the extent and range of conditions of the vast realm of space surrounding us, scientists think that there is a significant chance of life existing elsewhere—some would even say a virtual certainty. This is an interesting combination of ideas for your students to grapple with, and The Drake Equation helps students better understand the probability of life existing elsewhere.

What You Need

For the class:
- ❏ the Star Types chart from Activity 2
- ❏ 1 copy each of the Red Stars, Yellow Stars, White Stars, and Blue Stars sheets (masters on pages 118–121)
- ❏ 1 piece each of red, yellow, white, and blue paper
- ❏ 4 envelopes
- ❏ the overhead transparency of page 7 of the Message from Space from Activity 1, Session 2
- ❏ an overhead projector

For each team of 2–4 students:
- ❏ 1 piece of 11" x 17" paper
- ❏ 2 pencils
- ❏ 1 copy of The Distant Planetary System student sheet (master on page 122)
- ❏ 1 strip compass (or tape measure/ruler marked in centimeters)

For each strip compass:
- ❏ 1 copy of the Strip Compass student sheet (master on page 123)
- ❏ scissors
- ❏ glue or glue stick
- ❏ 1 pushpin
- ❏ a 2" x 18" strip of tagboard (or light cardboard)

Getting Ready

1. Copy the Red Stars sheet (master on page 118) onto red paper, the Yellow Stars sheet (master on page 119) onto yellow paper, the White Stars sheet (master on page 120) onto white paper, and the Blue Stars sheet (master on page 121) onto blue paper. If you do not have colored paper, you could use markers to color in the circles on these pages.

2. Cut out the stars roughly, by cutting them into squares. Each team can later carefully cut out the circles. Put each set of rough-cut stars into an envelope labeled with the star's color.

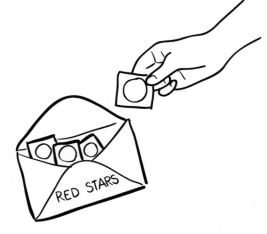

3. Make one copy of the Strip Compass (master on page 123) for each team and cut it out. Also make one copy of The Distant Planetary System sheet (master on page 122) for each team.

4. Add the following measurements for rocky planet zones and gas giant zones to the information on the Star Types chart.

Star Lifezones

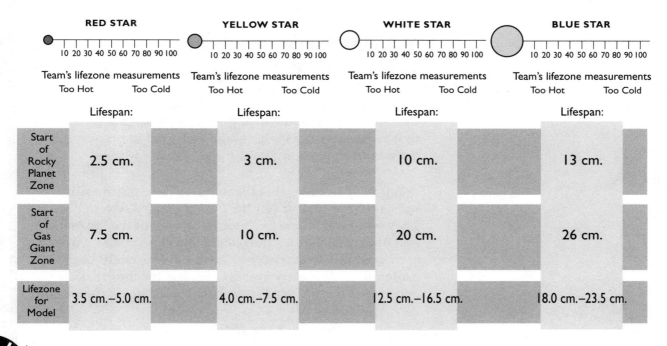

	RED STAR	YELLOW STAR	WHITE STAR	BLUE STAR
	10 20 30 40 50 60 70 80 90 100	10 20 30 40 50 60 70 80 90 100	10 20 30 40 50 60 70 80 90 100	10 20 30 40 50 60 70 80 90 100
	Team's lifezone measurements	Team's lifezone measurements	Team's lifezone measurements	Team's lifezone measurements
	Too Hot Too Cold	Too Hot Too Cold	Too Hot Too Cold	Too Hot Too Cold
	Lifespan:	Lifespan:	Lifespan:	Lifespan:
Start of Rocky Planet Zone	2.5 cm.	3 cm.	10 cm.	13 cm.
Start of Gas Giant Zone	7.5 cm.	10 cm.	20 cm.	26 cm.
Lifezone for Model	3.5 cm.–5.0 cm.	4.0 cm.–7.5 cm.	12.5 cm.–16.5 cm.	18.0 cm.–23.5 cm.

GO !

Introducing the Activity

1. Tell your students that, now that they have studied our solar system, they will try to imagine more about what the planetary system whose inhabitants sent the seven-page message from space is like.

2. Let students know that although they only have one example to work from, our solar system, they can assume that many of the rules may apply in other planetary systems as well. At the same time, they can also assume that there are a huge number of variations that can occur in different planetary systems!

3. Let students know that they will be using the planetary system that they design in this activity as a setting for a science fiction story they will write in a later activity.

4. Show the overhead transparency of the final page of the Message from Space (from Activity 1, Session 2). Point out the section at the top of the page, and remind students that it appears to be our solar system, with its nine planets.

5. Also point out the section at the bottom of the page, and remind the class that it appears to be the ETs' planetary system. Remind students that it appeared to have six planets, and that the message seemed to show that the fourth planet underwent some kind of drastic change.

Making the Planetary Systems Suitable for Life

1. Tell students that the only information they have about the planetary system where the message originated is what they can learn from the message and what they have learned from studying stars and planetary systems.

2. Tell your students that the message does not appear to indicate what type of star the ETs' planetary system has. They will need to use the information about the lifezones and lifespans of different types of stars they learned in an earlier activity to choose which type of star might be at the center of the planetary system. Review the information about stars on the Star Types chart posted in the classroom.

3. Point out that you have added information to the chart about where rocky planets and gas giant planets are generally found around different kinds of stars. They will need to mark off and label any life zones (places where liquid water can be found). Remind them that there may be other lifezones on moons of gas giants. You may want to mention again that this information reflects our solar system and that other planetary systems may vary in many ways.

4. Review the criteria the students used to search for possible locations of life in the solar system when they took the tour: Rocky surface/Liquid water/Enough gravity to hold an atmosphere and liquid water/A survivable atmosphere/A source of energy, such as sunlight or active volcanoes.

5. Point out that a planetary system suitable for life would also need to have no major interference from comets or asteroids, and a planetary orbit that would not cause too much fluctuation in temperature. Also point out that the

orbits need to be far enough apart so the planets will not crash into each other.

6. Show students the colored papers which they will use as the stars at the centers of their systems and ask them to trim them into circles when they choose one. Remind them that scientists think it took over 4 billion years for complex life to evolve on Earth, so they will need to choose a star that would last long enough for an advanced civilization to evolve.

7. Encourage students to be creative, yet realistic. Remind them that they do know that there is life in the planetary system, so their design should reflect conditions necessary to support life. As they design the planetary system, they should keep in mind what they've learned about where life might evolve and survive.

Encouraging Creative Variations

1. Encourage your students to brainstorm other potential variations they could make in their planetary systems, such as:

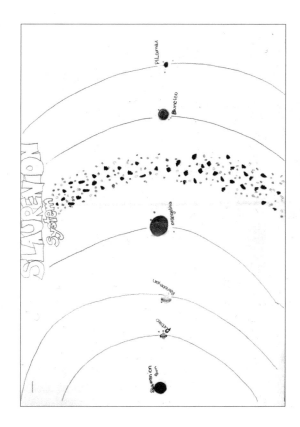

Asteroid belt(s): Our solar system has an asteroid belt between Mars and Jupiter. There is evidence that there may be another beyond Pluto. Does the ETs' planetary system have any asteroid belts? How did it (or they) form? Was it a collision of planets? Remember—too many asteroids could prevent conditions favorable to life.

Comet cloud: Scientists believe our solar system has a comet cloud far beyond Pluto, and that occasionally a comet breaks loose from the cloud and comes closer to the Sun. Does the ETs' planetary system have a comet cloud?

Moons: Many planets in our solar system have moons, some of which are large and potentially inhabitable, while others are very small. Do any of the planets in the ETs' planetary system have moons? How did they form? Did they break off from the planet? Are they "captured" asteroids? Did they form at the same time as the planet? Be sure that the moons have their own separate orbits, so they will not collide.

Dust rings: Saturn, Jupiter, Neptune, and Uranus all have dust rings. Do any of the planets in the distant planetary system have dust rings?

2. Mention that these are only a few examples and that there are many other possible variations. Students may have many other great ideas, based on their own unique interpretation of the message from space, their ideas for their science fiction stories, and their wonderfully creative imaginations!

Making and Using Strip Compasses

1. You may choose to use tape measures or rulers instead of strip compasses to measure the zones of the planetary systems. The advantage of the strip compass is that the students can more easily mark off the zones, and can also use them to draw the orbits of their planets and moons. Once the strip compasses are made, they can also be saved as a class set to use if you plan to teach the unit in the future.

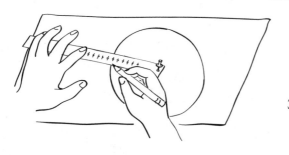

2. If you do not already have strip compasses, demonstrate how to make them. Draw each step on the board.

    a. Tape, glue, or paste the ruler strip onto the edge of the strip of tagboard.

    b. Use a pushpin to make a hole at the "0" point.

3. Demonstrate how to use the strip compass:

    a. Use a pushpin to make a hole in the strip compass large enough to accommodate the point of a pencil at the measurement you have chosen.

    b. Put the point of a sharp pencil through the "0" point on the compass and hold it down at the *center* of the star.

    c. Put the point of another pencil in the hole at the desired measurement.

    d. While holding the "0" point fixed with one pencil, make an arc with the other pencil.

4. Demonstrate to your students how to measure and mark how far the lifezones would extend. Demonstrate the

rocky planet and gas giant zones, using the strip compass. Tell them that they may also use the strip compass to draw the orbits of their planets and moons on the 11" x 17" paper.

5. Explain that for each planet in their systems they should draw an arc centered on the star to show the planet's orbit, and also draw the planet. The sizes of their drawings should indicate the relative sizes of the planets in their systems.

6. Point out that this model will not be to scale. The star size, the planet sizes, and the distances between the star and planets will all be at different scales.

7. Pass out the strip compasses, pencils, and sheets of 11" x 17" paper to the teams. Remind students of the location of the paper-circle stars.

Refecting on Models

1. When students have finished designing their planetary systems, distribute The Distant Planetary System student sheet for them to complete.

2. Tell your students that they have just created a hypothetical model using researched data available to them. Model making of this kind is a major part of the science of astronomy. The next step an astronomer might take would be to evaluate the accuracy of this model as more data comes in to see if the model still makes sense.

3. Since we are living in a period of continual discovery of new planetary systems, encourage your students to keep up with the news, and compare their models with newly discovered planetary systems. Who knows—their model may even predict some strange aspect of a planetary system that we will later find out actually does exist!

Note: Your students will need their planetary systems while writing their science fiction stories in Activity 6.

Critical Reading Assignment

1. A series of articles, modified and adapted from actual articles, are provided as a reading assignment for your students. (The names of the scientists in the scientifically accurate articles have been retained. The names of "scien-

You may want to have your students consider an article that appeared in the February 8, 2000 New York Times national Science/Health section entitled "Maybe We Are Alone in the Universe, After All." This summarizes the arguments contained in a book entitled Rare Earth *(published by Springer-Verlag in January 2000) by Peter D. Ward and Donald C. Brownlee to the effect that the Earth's composition and stability are exceedingly rare and that in most other places the combination of radiation, lack of certain chemical elements, lack of hospitable planets, and other destructive factors make the likelihood of extraterrestrial life forms much less likely than many scientists have previously assumed. The authors do not oppose further scientific investigation and in fact propose a number of searches to further evaluate their hypothesis, including continuation of radio searches for intelligent life and closer examination of Mars, Europa, Ganymede, and Titan for signs of microbes. Commenting on the book Dr. Frank Drake of the SETI Institute told the Times, "the basic flaw in all these arguments is that they don't allow for the opportunistic nature of life, its ability to accommodate or alter itself to cope with environmental change." The questions raised in the article are very interesting and would involve your students in considering many aspects of the sciences, including chemistry, plate tectonics, and evolution.*

*It is 26 trillion miles to the **nearest** star (aside from the Sun) and it takes four years for light, traveling at 186,000 miles per second, to travel that distance.*

tists" in the other tabloid-style articles are fictitious, as are the names of all of the article authors.)

2. You may want to assign the articles as homework and have a class discussion the next day. Ask students to decide which articles are serious and which are not—that is, which seem to be based on scientific thinking, and which are sensationalized fictions. While the distinction between the two is quite obvious upon a first reading, the idea here is less to pose a challenge than to help students see that with even a small amount of care, they should be able to recognize sensationalized fiction when they see it! **The unfortunate fact is that, as many surveys show, a large proportion of the population do not make this distinction.**

3. During the class discussion, here are some suggested questions to help elicit student reasoning about the articles:

• In analyzing the articles what "red flags" did you look for?

• What did you have a hard time believing. Why?

• What made an article believable to you? Why?

• Is information readily available in the article? Or does it state that information can't be revealed for one reason or another?

• Is the article vague or illogical?

• Is there credible confirmation offered for claims in the article?

• What about the writing style? Does it provide clues to the article's validity?

4. If students don't mention it, remind them of the vast distances involved and how unlikely it is that extraterrestrials could travel to Earth. As appropriate, point out that skepticism is an important element in science—scientists question their own work constantly and are skeptical about all claims unless they can be proven. Despite the multitude of claims of sightings and abductions, not one has ever been proven or confirmed.

The following articles are adapted and modified from real articles, some of which appeared in big city daily newspapers and others in tabloid-style publications. Which articles are serious, and which are not? Read them with a critical eye.

Is There Anybody Out There?

Radio Telescopes Seek Signals from Other Planets

By Vivian Milligan

There have been many "false alarms," but so far scientists say that they have not found any signs of extraterrestrial life. "It is, of course, only a start," said Peter Backus, of the Phoenix Project.

The Phoenix Project is a search organized by the SETI Institute. Using radio telescopes around the world, they are searching the skies for radio signals from intelligent extraterrestrials.

Although some scientists argue that the search is foolish, many serious astronomers say that detecting messages from intelligent extraterrestrials is very possible.

They argue that there probably is life on an Earth-like planet circling a star like our Sun. No one knows how many Earth-like planets there are, but because there are so many stars like our Sun, even in our own galaxy, these scientists say that the odds are that there might be many such planets.

The search is focused on stars that are like our Sun, and that are relatively nearby. In this case, "nearby" means within 200 light years distance, or, in other words, one quadrillion 200 trillion (1,200,000,000,000,000) miles away!

Radio signals can travel huge distances in space, although it can take hundreds of years for them to travel that far. On Earth, we've only had the technology to send radio signals for about one hundred years. In a few hundred years though, our radio and television signals could be picked up by an extraterrestrial listener many light years away.

Jill Tarter, Director of the SETI Institute, said, "It is the most important question the human species has asked itself...are we alone or are we not?"
For more information about Project Phoenix, see:

phoenix info@seti-inst.edu
http://www.seti.org

Aliens came here in a spaceship— and may have built the Pyramids!

Jungle Find! 15,000-year-old UFO!

Expert says ETs started a colony on Earth

By Kevin Erickson

Dr. Ivan Bergman would not reveal the exact location of the UFO.

MOSCOW - Russian scientists say they have found a 15,000-year-old spaceship in an African jungle—but that's not all. They also found strange metal documents at the site which claim the ETs later built a colony. This means that their descendants may be walking among us today!

Dr. Ivan Bergman says that the spaceship proves the ETs had the technology to reach our planet thousands of years before the Pyramids were built. He reported that the spaceship was found in the jungles of Kenya on October 27, but he would not pinpoint the exact location for "security reasons."

He also said the spaceship had been taken apart and shipped to Moscow for study. "It's in amazingly good condition, considering it's 15,000 years old!"

The documents have not been translated, but they include pictures of aliens living in pyramid-shaped huts. Bergman said, "We think that the fact that they built pyramid-shaped huts may mean that they also built the Pyramids thousands of years later."

In an exciting prediction, Dr. Bergman told reporters, "We may someday be able to make a copy of their spaceship, and travel to other parts of the galaxy too."

Scientists Discover a Solar System Like Ours

New Finding Makes Extraterrestrial Life More Likely

By Felicia Cort

Astronomers have found a distant planetary system much like our own. The system has a sun-like star orbited by three planets. The discovery was made by astronomers from San Francisco State University, Harvard, Colorado, and Australia.

Up until now, the only planetary systems found with stars like our Sun had just one planet. This discovery proves that there are other systems like ours out there, with more than one planet. Astronomers think that there are many, but this is the first time they've actually been able to find one.

The discovery "implies that planets can form more easily than we ever imagined, and that our Milky Way is teeming with planetary systems," said Dr. Debra Fischer, one of the astronomers. It's thought that extraterrestrial life is most likely to be found around stars that are similar to our Sun.

The star is called Upsilon Andromedae, and it is 44 light-years away. A light year is the distance light travels in a year, which is 6 trillion miles. It is orbited by three planets the size of Jupiter.

Since they are so far away, the planets are too small to be seen, even with our most powerful telescopes.

They were discovered by studying "wobbling" in the way Upsilon Andromedae moved. As they orbit the star, the gravitational pull of the three planets tugs on it, and make the star "wobble" slightly.

In our solar system, gas giants, such as Jupiter, Saturn, Uranus, and Neptune, formed much farther from the Sun than those around Upsilon Andromedae. Because until recently the only planets that could be studied have been our own nine, scientists had generally thought that gas giants could not form so close to a "yellow" star like our Sun.

R. Paul Butler and Geoffrey Marcy have been studying Upsilon Andromedae for 11 years. They discovered one planet in the system in 1996, before Fischer discovered the other two. Marcy said, "I am mystified as to how such a system of Jupiter-like planets might have been created." He added, "This will shake up the theory of planetary formation."

A map of the orbits of Upsilon Andromedae's three planets can be seen at www.physics.sfsu.edu/planetsearch.

Texas Woman Has Terrifying Encounter

'My Dog was Eaten by a Space Alien!'

Alien dog-eater! Jaine Barber holds up a picture of the alien that ate her poodle Fluffy, as drawn by an artist.

UFO researcher Len Willard

By
Dwight Duwigahut
Global News Agency

A 34-year-old Texas woman says she watched in horror as a space alien ate her dog Fluffy. Although her story may sound ridiculous, reports of other animal devourings have been coming in from certain areas of the world for months. These same spots have also had many recent UFO sightings.

"People may not believe me, but I swear it's true," said Miss Barber. "I heard a whirring sound, and the bushes in my backyard started blowing around. The next thing I knew, a flying saucer appeared overhead, and a lizard-like alien was lowered down.

"I started to run away, but it stared at me with glowing eyes, and I couldn't move. Just then Fluffy ran up to the alien wagging her tail. I was horrified that I couldn't move to help stop it from eating my little Fluffy."

Miss Barber described the alien as being about the size of a man, with green scales, a large tail, and a lizard-like head.

"After the alien ate Fluffy, it disappeared. The spaceship then started whirring, and then it disappeared too."

Miss Barber then called Huntsville-based UFO researcher Matthew Stone. Stone said "recently there have been dozens of sightings like this in Brazil, Florida, New Mexico, and Argentina."

Europa May Have Ingredients for Life

Water, energy and organic matter likely!

By Kimi Tucker

Instruments on the Galileo spacecraft, which is orbiting Jupiter, have discovered organic chemicals (the building blocks of life) on the moons Callisto and Ganymede, which are neighbors of Europa.

The chemicals are thought to have come from comets and meteorites. Although the chemicals have not yet been found on Europa, it is close by and could very well have them too.

It was already known that Europa has water and heat. If it also has organic chemicals, it is a strong candidate for life of some kind to have evolved.

"This doesn't mean there is life on Europa," said Dr. McCord, lead author of a study published in the journal *Science.* "The exciting thing now is the evidence that Europa may have all three of the ingredients."

To see if life could exist in icy conditions like those on Europa, scientists have been looking for places on Earth with similar conditions. In studying ice a mile deep in Antarctica, they have found primitive life forms 100,000 years old.

No organic chemicals have been found on Europa, but scientists think there may be a rich organic soup under its thick layer of ice. This could be a warm, liquid place where life could have evolved.

Flying Saucer Crash Site

34 Alien Corpses Found in Alien Spaceship in Siberia

By Lynn Sneider

YAKUTSK, Siberia - An alien spaceship was discovered in a huge block of ice in Siberia. This is already being hailed as the most important discovery in the history of the world!

According to Dr. Yuri Logoff, "Over the years there have been many UFO sightings and alien abductions reported—but now we finally have concrete evidence. This find is the first proof of life on other planets."

The strange-shaped flying saucer is made of a type of metal unlike anything found on Earth. It has a 60- foot diameter, and has strange bumps along the outside.

Most interesting of all, scientists used scanners to explore inside the craft, and found at least 34 alien bodies. Dr. Logoff says that it will take until mid-November 2003 to thaw them out.

Since the spacecraft seems unharmed, Dr. Logoff says that he thinks that the extraterrestrials may have run out of fuel, landed, and then starved to death, stranded in the ice.

He predicted, "When we've finished thawing out these aliens, we will shock the world!"

Special Going Further: The Drake Equation

This activity uses a mathematical equation to estimate the number of civilizations in the Milky Way Galaxy with whom we could potentially communicate. It is fun and instructive for the students to come up with their own estimates. It helps them ponder for themselves the important question of whether or not such communication is likely to occur. Of necessity, the equation is a series of estimates. By this point in the unit, students have some familiarity with the information needed to make these estimates. Depending on the grade level of your students, you may choose to work together and discuss, as a class, Steps 1–4, or more, of the student sheet. Students may work in teams of two, or individually, through the rest of the sheet. A blank copy of the two-page student sheet appears following this explanatory write-up. Duplicate it for your students and decide how you will work through it.

1. Tell your students that many people think the idea of communicating with extraterrestrials is ridiculous. Let students know that now that they have studied space and the requirements for life to evolve on other worlds, they'll take a look at whether or not it's likely.

2. Tell them that to find out if communication is likely, one important thing to consider is the number of civilizations in the galaxy right now with whom we might communicate. Unfortunately we don't know this, but we can make an estimate. Tell your students that with a step-by-step equation they will make **their own** estimate concerning the chances that someone out there really might be sending messages to us or able to receive our messages.

Frank Drake, the "father" of SETI, proposed the Drake equation in 1960. It first appeared as the agenda for a scientific meeting to discuss the likelihood that SETI searches would make a discovery of extraterrestrial intelligence.

You may want to point out that placing a zero (0) in any box on the Drake Equation sheet will result in there being zero civilizations—no intelligence—including ourselves!

THE DRAKE EQUATION

Should we be sending messages into space? Is it very likely that we might receive a message from space? Use the Drake Equation to help you make your own estimate of the number of civilizations in the Milky Way Galaxy that may exist now. Read each step and write your estimate in the box to the right.

1. Number of stars in our galaxy: 400 billion (400,000,000,000)

Although we can't be sure, most astronomers agree that this number is probably a good estimate.

Divide this number by:

2. Lifetime of our galaxy: about 10 billion years (10,000,000,000)

Write the number in the box.

3. The average rate of turnover of stars per year.

Some stars last a long time, others are more short-lived. On an average, this is the number of stars that are born and that die per year.

You may want to review lifespans of stars from Activity 2. Your students may also need help dividing such large numbers. You may choose to show them how to eliminate zeros to simplify the problem, or you may choose to simply give them the number 40 as the answer.

4. Fraction of stars with long enough lifespans for intelligent life to evolve.

It took about 5 billion years after our Sun formed for intelligent life with the technology to communicate through space to evolve on Earth. If we call 5 billion years the minimum amount of time needed, then what fraction of the 400 billion stars do you think has a lifespan of 5 billion years or more?

| all = 1.0 | 3/4 = 0.75 | 1/2 = 0.5 | 1/4 = 0.25 | other |

Write your estimate in decimals in the box.

5. Average number of planets per star.

Our solar system has 9 planets. Our Sun is considered an average star. What do you think the *average* number of planets around stars is?

| 20 | 10 | 5 | other |

Write the number in the box.

You may want to remind your students that most stars probably are binary stars (2 stars together) or more.

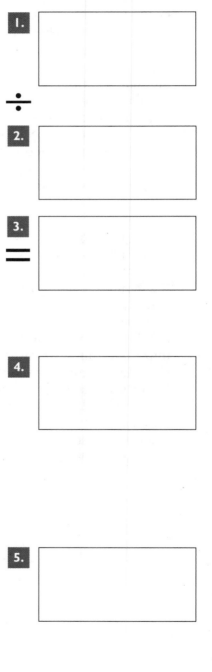

6. Fraction of planets suitable for life.

In our solar system, out of nine planets, Earth is the only one known to be in the lifezone, and Mars almost is. Some astronomers also argue that there may be lifezones on some moons around gas giants. If we only count Earth, the fraction of planets in the lifezone of our star is 1/9 or 0.11. Of the planets around other stars, what fraction do you think are in a lifezone?

1/4 = 0.25   1/10 = 0.1   1/40 = .025   1/50 = .02   1/100 = .01   other

Write the decimal in the box.

7. Fraction of planets suitable for life, where life actually does occur.

Earth is the only example we have of a planet in a lifezone, and life *did* evolve. What fraction of planets in lifezones do you think would evolve life?

all = 1.0   3/4 = 0.75   1/2 = 0.5   1/4 = 0.25   1/8 = 0.125   other

Write the decimal in the box.

8. Fraction of planets with life that develop intelligent civilizations.

Earth is the only example we have of a planet that evolved life, and on Earth, intelligent civilizations have developed. What fraction of planets with life do you think would develop intelligent civilizations?

all = 1.0   3/4 = 0.75   1/2 = 0.5   1/4 = 0.25   1/8 = 0.125   other

Write the decimal in the box.

You may want to remind your students that Earth has had huge die-offs from asteroids or other catastrophic events about every 26 million years. Would one of these catastrophes destroy a civilized species or not?

9. The average lifespan of civilizations with the technology and desire to communicate through space.

This one is the hardest to estimate. The average lifespan of stars suitable for life is 5–10 billion years. On Earth, we only developed the technology to communicate through space during the last 100 years. Do you think our civilization could last 5 billion years, or do you think it will end before then? Now, what about the *average* civilization in our galaxy?

1,000 years   10,000 years   1,000,000 years   1,000,000,000 years   5,000,000,000 years   other

Write the number in the box.

Multiply the numbers in boxes 3–9.

10. This number is your own personal estimate of the number of civilizations in the Milky Way Galaxy right now with whom we might communicate.

10.

11. Look at the number you ended up with, and think about your result. Do you think there is much chance we might pick up a message from an extraterrestrial civilization if we listen?

12. Do you think we should be trying to communicate with extraterrestrial civilizations or not? Why or why not?

13. Remember that you just estimated how many intelligent civilizations there may be in our galaxy, but there are billions of galaxies in the Universe. How many civilizations in the *Universe* do you think there are right now with whom we might communicate?

14. There may be planets where life has evolved, but it has NOT reached an intelligent enough level to communicate through space. How many such planets do you think there are in our galaxy?

15. Compare your result with a classmate's. If they are very different, try to figure out why.

16. Since the final estimate is the hardest and has the most chance of being inaccurate, you may want to try changing it to see how the change affects the outcome.

THE DRAKE EQUATION

Should we be sending messages into space? Is it very likely that we might receive a message from space? Use the Drake Equation to help you make your own estimate of the number of civilizations in the Milky Way Galaxy that may exist now. Read each step and write your estimate in the box to the right.

1. Number of stars in our galaxy: 400 billion (400,000,000,000)

Although we can't be sure, most astronomers agree that this number is probably a good estimate.

Divide this number by:

2. Lifetime of our galaxy: about 10 billion years (10,000,000,000)

Write the number in the box.

3. The average rate of turnover of stars per year.

Some stars last a long time, others are more short-lived. On an average, this is the number of stars that are born and that die per year.

4. Fraction of stars with long enough lifespans for intelligent life to evolve.

It took about 5 billion years after our Sun formed for intelligent life with the technology to communicate through space to evolve on Earth. If we call 5 billion years the minimum amount of time needed, then what fraction of the 400 billion stars do you think has a lifespan of 5 billion years or more?

all = 1.0   3/4 = 0.75   1/2 = 0.5   1/4 = 0.25   other

Write your estimate in decimals in the box.

5. Average number of planets per star.

Our solar system has 9 planets. Our Sun is considered an average star. What do you think the *average* number of planets around stars is?

20   10   5   other

Write the number in the box.

6. Fraction of planets suitable for life.

In our solar system, out of nine planets, Earth is the only one known to be in the lifezone, and Mars almost is. Some astronomers also argue that there may be lifezones on some moons around gas giants. If we only count Earth, the fraction of planets in the lifezone of our star is 1/9 or 0.11. Of the planets around other stars, what fraction do you think are in a lifezone?

1/4 = 0.25   1/10 = 0.1   1/40 = .025   1/50 = .02   1/100 = .01   other

Write the decimal in the box.

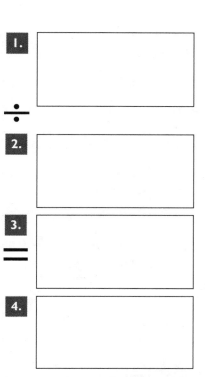

7. Fraction of planets suitable for life, where life actually does occur.

Earth is the only example we have of a planet in a lifezone, and life *did* evolve. What fraction of planets in lifezones do you think would evolve life?

all = 1.0   3/4 = 0.75   1/2 = 0.5   1/4 = 0.25   1/8 = 0.125   other

Write the decimal in the box.

7. [ ]

8. Fraction of planets with life that develop intelligent civilizations.

Earth is the only example we have of a planet that evolved life, and on Earth, intelligent civilizations have developed. What fraction of planets with life do you think would develop intelligent civilizations?

all = 1.0   3/4 = 0.75   1/2 = 0.5   1/4 = 0.25   1/8 = 0.125   other

Write the decimal in the box.

8. [ ]

9. The average lifespan of civilizations with the technology and desire to communicate through space.

This one is the hardest to estimate. The average lifespan of stars suitable for life is 5–10 billion years. On Earth, we only developed the technology to communicate through space during the last 100 years. Do you think our civilization could last 5 billion years, or do you think it will end before then? Now, what about the *average* civilization in our galaxy?

1,000 years   10,000 years   1,000,000 years   1,000,000,000 years   5,000,000,000 years   other

Write the number in the box. Multiply the numbers in boxes 3–9.

9. [ ]

10. This number is your own personal estimate of the number of civilizations in the Milky Way Galaxy right now with whom we might communicate.

10. [ ]

11. Look at the number you ended up with, and think about your result. Do you think there is much chance we might pick up a message from an extraterrestrial civilization if we listen?

12. Do you think we should be trying to communicate with extraterrestrial civilizations or not? Why or why not?

13. Remember that you just estimated how many intelligent civilizations there may be in our galaxy, but there are billions of galaxies in the Universe. How many civilizations in the *Universe* do you think there are right now with whom we might communicate?

14. There may be planets where life has evolved, but it has NOT reached an intelligent enough level to communicate through space. How many such planets do you think there are in our galaxy?

15. Compare your result with a classmate's. If they are very different, try to figure out why.

16. Since the final estimate is the hardest and has the most chance of being inaccurate, you may want to try changing it to see how the change affects the outcome.

Astronomers See New Planet's Shadow Cross A Distant Star

By Robert Sanders
PUBLIC AFFAIRS

"This is the first independent confirmation of a planet discovered through changes in a star's radial velocity and demonstrates that our indirect evidence for planets really is due to planets,"

Geoffrey Marcy, professor of astronomy

Astronomers have witnessed for the first time a distant planet passing in front of its star, providing direct and independent confirmation of the existence of extrasolar planets that to date have been inferred only from the wobble of their star.

"This is the first independent confirmation of a planet discovered through changes in a star's radial velocity and demonstrates that our indirect evidence for planets really is due to planets," said Geoffrey Marcy, professor of astronomy.

Marcy and his colleagues, Paul Butler of the Department of Terrestrial Magnetism at the Carnegie Institution of Washington in Washington, D.C., and Steve Vogt of UC Santa Cruz and Lick Observatory, first detected a wobble in the star called HD 209458 on Nov. 5. Ascribing the wobble to a nearby planet, they were able to estimate its orbit and approximate mass.

As with all new planets they detect, the team immediately brought it to the attention of collaborator Greg Henry, an astronomer at the Tennessee State University Center of Excellence in Information Systems in Nashville. He conducts research with several automatic telescopes at Fairborn Observatory, a non-profit research foundation located in the Patagonia Mountains of southern Arizona.

Henry turned one of his automatic

© 1999 Lynette Cook

A team of scientists discovered a planet roughly 153 light years away.

telescopes on the star at the time Marcy and Butler predicted the planet would cross the face of the star if the planet's orbital plane were lucky enough to carry it between Earth and the star. Until now, none of the 18 other extrasolar planets Marcy and Butler have discovered has had its orbital plane oriented edge-on to Earth so that the planet could be seen to transit the star, nor have any of the other planets discovered by other researchers.

However, on Nov. 7, Henry observed a 1.7 percent dip in the star's brightness. "This planetary transit occurred at

exactly the time predicted from Marcy's observations, confirming absolutely the presence of a companion," Henry said. "The amount of dimming of the star's light during the transit also gives us the first-ever measure of the size and density of an extrasolar planet. We've essentially seen the shadow of the planet and used it to measure the planet's size."

The star HD 209458 is 153 light years or or 859,000 billion miles away in the constellation of Pegasus, and is about the same age, color and size as our own sun. It is very near the star. 51

Pegasi, around which the first extrasolar planet was discovered in 1995.

With the orbital plane of the planet known, the astronomers for the first time could determine precisely the mass of the planet and, from the size of the planet measured during transit, its density.

Interestingly, while the planet's mass is only 63 percent of Jupiter's mass, its radius is 60 percent bigger than that of Jupiter. This fits with theories that predict a bloated planet when, as here, the planet is very close to the star.

The density, about 0.2 grams per cubic centimeter, means it is a gas giant like Jupiter. However, such gas giants could not have formed at the distance this planet is from its star.

"This supports the theory that extrasolar planets very near their star did not form where they are, but formed farther out and migrated inward," Henry said.

Various groups around the world have been searching for planets by looking for dimming of stars, or as Marcy says, "staring at the sky and seeing if any star blinks." To date, none of these searches has turned up a new planet.

"With this one, everything hangs together," Marcy said. "This is what we've been waiting for."

More information on the artist rendering can be found at (www. spaceart. org/lcook/extrasol.html).

RED STARS

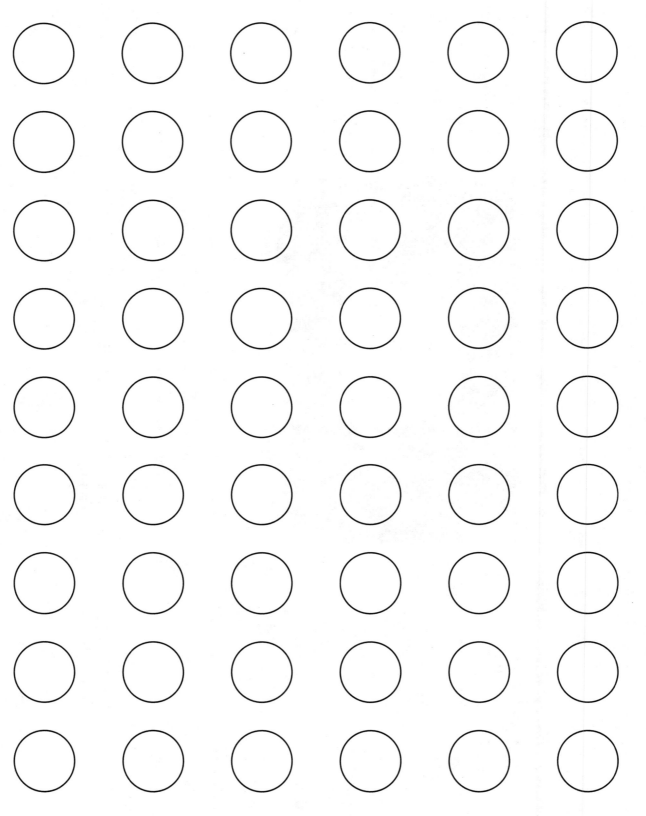

Yellow Stars

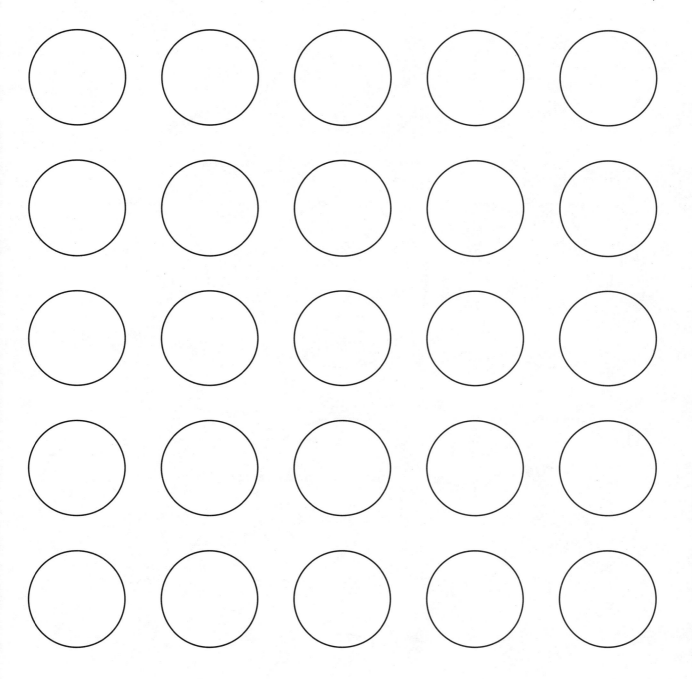

White Stars

BLUE STARS

THE DISTANT PLANETARY SYSTEM

1. Our star is named Sol, and our planetary system is called the solar system. What is the name of your star and planetary system?

Star:_____   Planetary System:_____

2. List the names of your planets and describe each one, including gravity, presence of water, atmosphere (if it has one), temperature, surface, and whether or not it has moons.

3. If your planetary system has asteroid belts and/or a comet cloud, explain how they formed.

4. Where is there life in your planetary system, and where did it first evolve?

STRIP COMPASS MASTER

1. Cut a strip of tag board at least 1 ¹/₂" by 16".
2. Cut out the two parts of the ruler.
3. Glue pieces of the ruler to the tag board so that the tips of te arrows line up.
4. Use a push pin to poke a hole at the zero point.

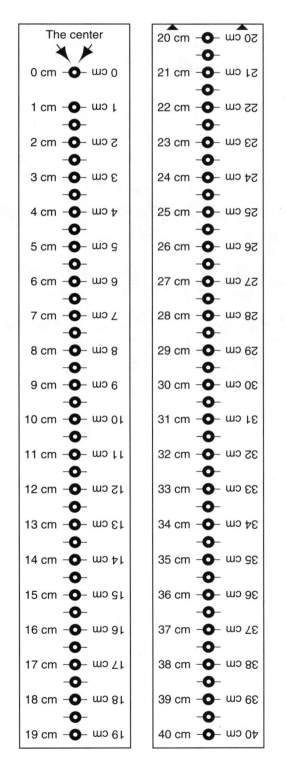

STRIP COMPASS MASTER

1. Cut a strip of tag board at least 1 ¹/₂" by 16".
2. Cut out the two parts of the ruler.
3. Glue pieces of the ruler to the tag board so that the tips of te arrows line up.
4. Use a push pin to poke a hole at the zero point.

Activity 6: Science Fiction Stories

"Not one of those worlds will be identical to Earth. A few will be hospitable; most will appear hostile. Many will be achingly beautiful. In some worlds there will be many Suns in the daytime sky, many moons in the heavens at night, or great particle ring systems soaring from horizon to horizon. Some moons will be so close that their planet will loom high in the heavens, covering half the sky. And some worlds will look out onto a vast gaseous nebula, the remains of an ordinary star that once was and is no longer."

Carl Sagan, Cosmos

Overview

In this activity, students write science fiction stories about the lifeforms who sent the message received in Activity 1. In teams or independently, they first use the Science Fiction Ideas sheet to plan their stories, imagine what it's like on the ETs' planet, and flesh out their characters. They then use these ideas to write their science fiction stories. You may go further and have students present their stories as plays or videos.

This assignment is a powerful language arts activity, and it can also be assessed according to science curriculum criteria. Students build upon what they've learned in the unit to create their story. A suggested rubric for assessing the stories as a science assignment is included on page 130.

Science teachers and language arts teachers may wish to collaborate on this assignment to strengthen the link between science learning and writing. Using this activity as a combined assignment for two classes is also a way to make available more class time and homework time. Teachers in multi-subject self-contained classrooms can integrate two subjects in their classrooms with this activity.

What You Need

- ☐ the ET planetary systems from Activity 5
- ☐ 1 copy of the Science Fiction Ideas sheet (master on page 129) per student or team

Getting Ready

1. Decide whether you want students to work independently or in teams.

2. Duplicate one copy of the Science Fiction Ideas sheet (master on page 129) per student or team.

3. Place the student models of extraterrestrial planetary systems so every student from the team can examine them while working on their stories.

Talking about Science Fiction

·1. Ask students to share brief comments about **science fiction** books, movies, or TV shows they've enjoyed. Ask them to think about what made these stories good. Explain that, in this closing activity of the unit, they will write science fiction stories about the distant lifeforms that sent the seven-page Message from Space.

2. Add that the best science fiction stories are strange and different from what we're used to, but also have realistic elements with well-thought-out scientific details. Remind students that they used science to design their planetary systems. These planetary systems may be very different from our solar system, but **perhaps some of the systems they made up could actually exist.** Remind them that the systems they designed will serve as the settings for their stories.

3. Tell students their stories may be as strange as they want, but that they should try to show in their stories how these strange things *could actually happen in their distant world.* You may want to strongly suggest that they avoid a story line in which ETs travel to Earth because traveling across such huge distances in space is considered impossible (at this point in time). If their story includes migration from one planet to another they should describe the method the ETs used to travel over great distances.

4. If you want to give students some examples of how to work descriptions of their distant settings into their stories, try reading the following passages aloud. After each passage, ask them what kind of place the story is set in.

- I went to visit my friend. It took me a long time to get there.

- I went to visit my friend. The streets were crowded and I had to wait at every traffic light.

- I went to visit my friend. There were so many wildflowers along the path that I just had to stop and pick some.

- I went to visit my friend. The weather report said it might rain so of course I took the time to put on my acid protection gear before I left.

- I went to visit my friend. Halfway there I had to duck into a cave because the Suns were rising and the rocks were burning my flippers. A short time later, after the Suns had gone down again, I hurried on my way.

If you have time, as a group activity, have students suggest more reasons that it took so long to visit the friend, while including language describing or implying the setting.

Planning the Stories

1. Tell students that many great stories have only a few main characters, with one lead character, from whose perspective the story is told. Remind them of the vague story line hinted at in the message.

2. Let students know that they could choose to tell the story of what happened to the planet, and why the extra-terrestrials sent the message. They could also choose to write about what happened when the distant lifeforms received a reply to their message from Earth. They could write a story of some other huge event in the planetary system, or they could just tell a story involving the every-day life of an extraterrestrial.

3. Ask students to imagine that they are on a planet that supports life in the planetary system they designed. En-courage them to think about what it looks, smells, and

feels like. Ask them to imagine what the extraterrestrials are like. You may want to read them all or part of the Carl Sagan quotation from his book *Cosmos*:

> "Not one of those worlds will be identical to Earth. A few will be hospitable; most will appear hostile. Many will be achingly beautiful. In some worlds there will be many Suns in the day-time sky, many moons in the heavens at night, or great particle ring systems soaring from horizon to horizon. Some moons will be so close that their planet will loom high in the heavens, covering half the sky. And some worlds will look out onto a vast gaseous nebula, the remains of an ordinary star that once was and is no longer."

4. With the entire class, go through the questions listed on the Science Fiction Ideas sheet clarifying, if necessary, and encouraging brainstorming of creative ideas.

5. Distribute the Science Fiction Ideas sheet, one for each team, or one for each student if your students will be working individually. You may want to have students complete the assignment during one period, or you may want them to work on the Science Fiction Ideas sheet during one period, then write their stories in another class period, or as homework.

6. Go over the "Suggested Rubric" on page 130, so students will know the criteria on which their stories will be evaluated.

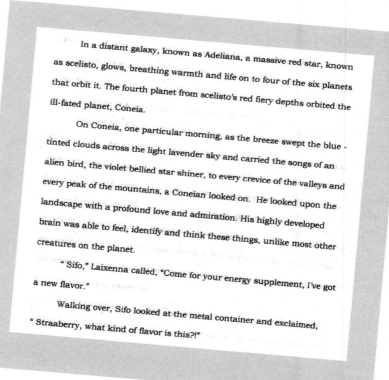

In a distant galaxy, known as Adeliana, a massive red star, known as scelisto, glows, breathing warmth and life on to four of the six planets that orbit it. The fourth planet from scelisto's red fiery depths orbited the ill-fated planet, Coneia.

On Coneia, one particular morning, as the breeze swept the blue-tinted clouds across the light lavender sky and carried the songs of an alien bird, the violet bellied star shiner, to every crevice of the valleys and every peak of the mountains, a Coneian looked on. He looked upon the landscape with a profound love and admiration. His highly developed brain was able to feel, identify and think these things, unlike most other creatures on the planet.

"Sifo," Laixenna called, "Come for your energy supplement, I've got a new flavor."

Walking over, Sifo looked at the metal container and exclaimed, "Straaberry, what kind of flavor is this?!"

Name(s): _____

Science Fiction Ideas

1. What is the name of the planet?

2. What is the atmosphere like? What does the sky look like?

3. What are the days, years, and seasons like?

4. What is the surface of the planet like—water, ice, land?

5. What kinds of animals and plants live there?

6. What are the intelligent creatures like?

7. What and how do they eat?

8. How do they breathe?

9. How do they communicate?

10. How do they protect themselves from the elements?

11. Do they have any enemies?

12. Are there natural disasters they have to deal with?

13. Do they have families? How do they reproduce?

14. Do they live underwater or on land?

15. What kind of music, art, sports, and/or entertainment do they have?

16. Do they have countries and/or governments? Do they have wars?

17. What were they trying to tell us in their message?

18. Who is the main character in your story?

19. What is your main character like?

20. What is the story you're going to tell?

21. What other characters are in the story?

22. Briefly make a plan for your story, including beginning, middle, and ending. Use the other side of this page if necessary.

You may want to convert major elements of these criteria into a student assignment sheet so students can refer to it as they write and refine their stories.

Suggested Rubric for Assessment of Stories as a Science Activity

The following are quality criteria:

- Student includes some descriptions of the ETs' planet, including:

  - what kind of star is at the center of the planetary system
  - where the planet is in the star's lifezone
  - what kind of surface the planet has
  - other conditions that make lifeforms possible

- The student shows how the extraterrestrials are physically adapted to its planet.

- The student describes how the behavior of the ETs in the story relates to the environment in which the story is set.

- The student compares and contrasts the ETs' environment to our solar system, including conditions on Earth and other planets.

- The student demonstrates understanding of the conditions thought necessary for life to exist.

- If the student's story includes migration from one planet to another, or even to another star system or to Earth, the story should demonstrate an understanding of the great distances involved in such a migration and explain how such distances were traversed.

Hello, my name is Blup. I'm here to tell you about life on my world, Pornge. I myself look rather different than you might imagine, with purple and orange swirled hair that stands at a towering two feet. I'm quite a sight to see for those of you on earth, but here on Pornge I'm perfectly normal.

My body is shaped like a pear, smaller on the top and larger on the hump on my rump. There [are] my tenticles, that are fuzzy & soft, which I use to scury into my mitter. A mitter is like a bucket with wheels that you call a car. Everyone has mittes, it is our transportation. They glide over tracks that are on Pornge. If you are rich you can use your mitter to go to the moons, Bornge & Bip. While using your mitter you can have the pleasure of going shopping, dining, playing or eating.

Our houses are small four stories and all we usually have eight people in the family not including our pets. The pets vary from land to land. Where I live cucino are the most common. Cucino have three legs, one foot, with five claws are on each leg. They have soft fur that varies in color from white to brown. They have pretty good

Chunkaloos and Venderschnots

...during these battles.

...So that is a brief description of what life on Bigums Le Ringums is like...

The Chunkaloos and the Venderschnots live on the planet Bigums Le Ringums. Their planet has eight moons and its many rings are made of plastic and green moon cheese. There is a lot of acid rain on Bigums Le Ringums, so the cities have protective domes over them. The atmosphere is very dense and the sky is rainbow swirled. There are no plants or animals other than the two mentioned species on the planet.

Behind the Scenes

Binary Code, Computer Images, and Digital TV

The pictures that the students create and examine in this unit are the simplest form of binary code. Each picture is a rectangle and each square in the rectangle is one small piece of the picture. The smallest piece of such a picture is called a *pixel*. Each bit in the computer message tells whether each pixel is "on" or "off."

On a computer monitor or on the screen of a digital TV set, the picture is also made of pixels, however the code for these computer and TV pictures is more complex. The code for each pixel must have many bits to carry the information about the color and brightness of the pixel.

Any civilization that has the technology to send and receive radio signals could probably figure out how to form an accurate picture from a message that uses only one bit for each pixel.

Distances in Space

Astronomers use a variety of distance measures, such as:

Astronomical Unit—The average distance from the Sun to the Earth; about 93 million miles, or 150 million kilometers. It is a good unit to measure distances within a planetary system, such as the solar system.

Light year—The distance light travels through empty space in one year; about 6 trillion miles, or 10 trillion kilometers. Light years are used to describe any of the largest distances in the universe. Smaller distances can be described as light minutes or light seconds. The Moon is about 1.5 light seconds from Earth. The Sun is about 8.3 light minutes from Earth. Since all electro-magnetic signals, such as radio waves or laser beams, travel at the speed of light, describing a distance in light years also describes how long a signal takes to travel that distance. For instance, the nearest star is over 4 light years away, so a radio message would take over four years to reach that star.

Parsec—About 3.26 light years. Parsec is short for parallax of one second. Parallax is an apparent shift in the position of an object when seen from two different

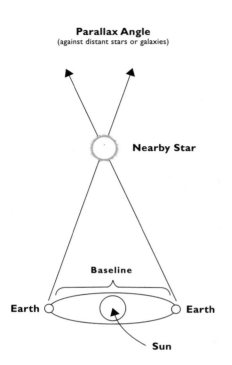

Parallax Angle
(against distant stars or galaxies)

Nearby Star

Baseline

Earth

Earth

Sun

points of view. This book, for example looks slightly different from your right eye and your left eye. Careful measurements of parallax shifts can be used to calculate the distance of an object. The distance to some of the closest stars in the Milky Way Galaxy can be found by looking at the stars in the spring, and then by looking again in the fall when the Earth has traveled half way around the Sun and is two Astronomical Units from its springtime position. An object that is 1 parsec away will appear to shift one second of arc ($\frac{1}{3600}$ of a degree) when observed from two places that are two AU apart. Since the measurement of all large distances in space depends on the accurate parallax measurement of close stars, the parsec (or sometimes the megaparsec) is a natural choice of measurement for distant objects.

About Radiometers

The Crookes radiometer is an ideal device for detecting radiant energy. Its spin is due to the heating power of the light that shines on it and it is not affected by the temperature of the surrounding air.

Within the radiometer are the vanes, four small thin sheets of material that are colored black on one side and white on the other. The dark sides of the vanes absorb the light that shines on them and thus warm up. The white sides reflect the light and stay slightly cooler. The more light that shines on the vanes, the greater the difference in temperature between the white surface and the black surface of each vane.

The glass bulb that surrounds the vanes has had the air pumped out of it, but not entirely. If there were a complete vacuum in the radiometer it would not work. The little bit of air that is in the radiometer gets heated slightly where it comes in contact with the warmer black surfaces of vanes. This warmer air gives the vanes of the radiometer a push, which causes the radiometer to spin.

As radiometers get old, air may leak into them. They may spin more slowly. This will affect the lifezone measurements in Activity 2.

See the end of the "Resources" section for instructions on how to make your own radiometer.

Solar System Formation

The theory that the solar system, and stars in general, formed from clouds of dust and gases has been the prevailing scientific view for almost two centuries. In the twentieth century, discoveries about the materials that planets are made from and increased knowledge about other bodies, such as asteroids and comets, have provided more clues to how the formation of the solar system took place.

Based upon our solar system, here is a simplified summary of the current theory of how planetary system formation occurs:

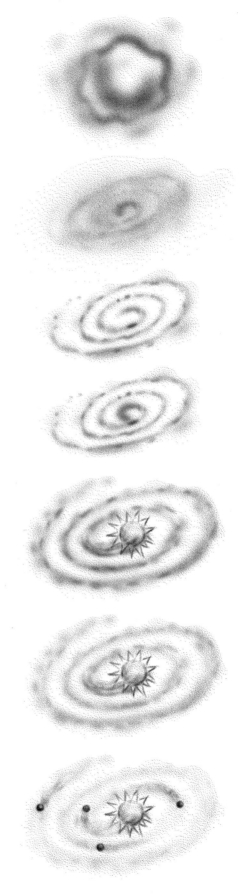

1. In space between the stars, gas and dust collects. Gravity pulls all matter together, so any collection of gas and dust would tend to collect more gas and dust. Originally there were only the gases hydrogen and helium, which were a direct product of the origin of the Universe—the so-called Big Bang. By the time our Sun was forming, space was filled with the remnants of stars that had already lived and died. Within these stars heavy elements were formed and were scattered through space whenever a particularly big star exploded. Some of the cloud that formed the solar system came from this material.

2. It would be extremely unlikely for all the dust and gas to fall evenly toward the center of the cloud. Instead the material ends up swirling around the middle of the cloud, something like water swirling as it approaches a drain. The cloud becomes a disk of swirling hot matter. The Hubble Telescope has seen such disks in the Orion Nebula, where new stars, and probably planets too, are forming.

3. In the center of the swirling disk, matter becomes so thick and hot that a reaction called nuclear fusion occurs. This reaction provides the energy that changes a lump of matter into a shining star. For the first part of its life this new star still lives in a hot disk of swirling material.

4. In the regions near the new star, lightweight materials, such as the gases that form air and water, are still too hot to clump together. Only the heavier materials, such as the elements that form rock and metal, begin to form chunks that orbit around the star. Over time these

chunks collect together to form rocky planets such as Mercury, Venus, Earth, and Mars.

5. Farther from the star, where it is cooler, the gas, ice, and dust gather to form giant gas planets, like Jupiter, Saturn, Uranus, and Neptune. These planets are made of the same kind of materials as our Sun. If any of them had been large enough (about 70 times larger than Jupiter) our solar system might have had another Sun.

6. Eventually the solar wind—streams of particles that flow away from a star—sweeps most of the remaining material right out of the system. What is left is the star itself, the nearby rocky planets, the more distant gas giant planets, and a variety of leftovers such as comets and asteroids.

7. Asteroids are chunks of rocks that end up in paths where they rarely encounter a planet or each other. Zones where most asteroids are concentrated are called asteroid belts. Our solar system has a major asteroid belt between the orbits of Mars and Jupiter. There is another one beyond Neptune. Gravity and collisions can send asteroids out of their belts, so there are no asteroid-free zones.

8. Comets are chunks of ice and rock that were flung out to the fringes of the solar system when the planets and asteroids were being formed. As long as comets remain far from the star they are cold and dark. Comets that fall back in toward the star heat up and form a bright cloud of gas and dust around themselves and often a tail. Comets that collided with the Earth probably provided the material for the oceans and the atmosphere, which were absent during the Earth's hot period of formation.

The current theories of the formation still leave many unanswered questions. Where do moons come from? How are systems of rings around planets formed? What about Pluto? What else is out there in the darkness far from the Sun?

The Big Bang

The "Big Bang" theory is about the history of the universe. Many discoveries in astronomy, subatomic physics, relativity and quantum theory support it. According to this mind-boggling theory, approximately 12-20 billion years ago, all matter and energy in the universe was compressed into a size much smaller than an atomic nucleus. Within a billionth of a second, whatever force was holding it all together transformed into the four forces known today (see below). Matter and energy began expanding at an enormous rate. Within three minutes, atomic nuclei formed. After about a million years, the universe had cooled down to the point where complete atoms formed. The galaxies, which formed about 2 billion years later, all continue to move apart today, as the universe continues to expand.

The Four Forces

The four forces that scientists classify in nature are:

Gravity—The attraction between any objects that have mass. It is the weakest of the forces, but has infinite range.

Electromagnetism—The attraction between charged particles such as electrons and protons. It is the second strongest force, and also has infinite range. Electricity is the result of this force.

Weak nuclear force—An attraction between nuclear particles that binds certain ones together. For example, weak force is what binds a proton with an electron in a neutron.

Strong nuclear force—holds protons and neutrons together. It is the strongest of the forces, but has very little range.

Within the first billionth of a second after the universe began, the four forces may have been united in a single unified force that held all matter and energy in the universe together.

We Are Stardust

Judging by the age of the oldest stars in our galaxy, it is calculated that our galaxy is 12–15 billion years old. Our Sun is "only" about 5 billion years old. The earliest stars were made from hydrogen and helium, which are light elements. Many larger stars explode at the end of their lives in huge supernova explosions. Heavy elements are produced in these explosions, so exploded stars send heavier elements out into space. Our Sun is not a first generation star, and our solar system contains these heavier elements. Each of us, and all that's around us, are all made from the stardust left over from stars that exploded!

Star Color

The color of a star is determined by its temperature. In the activity, "Star Types and Lifezones," students consider four types of stars—red, yellow, white, and blue. Astronomers define seven types of stars which they have labeled with the letters shown on the following chart, with O the hottest and M the coolest.

Spectral Letter	Temperature		Color
O	more than 37,000 F	(more than 20,500 C)	blue
B	17,000 - 37,000 F	(9,430 - 20,500 C)	blue-white
A	12,500 - 17,000 F	(6,930 - 9,430 C)	white
F	10,300 - 12,500 F	(5,700 - 6,930 C)	yellowish white
G	8,000 - 10,300 F	(4,400 - 5,700 C)	yellowish
K	5,500 - 8,000 F	(3,040 - 4,400 C)	orange
M	less than 5,500	(less than 3,040 C)	reddish

Although our Sun is a yellow "G" type star (close to 10,000 F), it will change during its "life cycle," as its nuclear fuel runs out. Near the end of its life, it will likely become a red giant, then later a very dense white dwarf. A red star we see in the sky may simply be a small red star, but it could also be the red giant phase of a star like our Sun. Hotter (type O) stars are blue and have different phases in their "lifecycle." "Blue giant" stars, at the end of their lifetimes, explode as supernovae and end up either as black holes (if they're really large) or as neutron stars. Some neutron stars, called pulsars, rotate and we see pulses of radio waves, like a giant radio lighthouse (such as the LGM's discovered in 1967 mentioned in the messages activity).

Black holes are invisible, because their gravitational pull is so strong that even light cannot escape. Neutron stars and white dwarfs become invisible as they cool over time. There are exceptions, however. These star "remnants" can be "rejuvenated" if their gravity attracts enough material from another nearby star.

A brown dwarf is a "failed star" that forms from a gas cloud that doesn't have enough material to condense and get hot enough for nuclear fusion to begin. They are detected mostly through infrared radiation.

Supernova

If a star is born with a mass much greater than our Sun's, it will end its lifespan with an enormous explosion called a supernova. Toward the end of a star's life, it has an iron core smaller than the size of the Earth (Earth is about 8,000 miles in diameter), but with more mass than our Sun. Iron cannot burn in a nuclear reaction, and when nuclear burning ends, the iron core suddenly collapses to a diameter of only about 12 miles! An inconceivable amount of energy is released—the same amount that 100 "Sun-like" stars release over 10 billion years! These supernova are so bright they can easily be seen from another galaxy, millions of light years away! The gravity of the remnants of the star may be so great that particles and light cannot escape from it, and it is called a black hole. It could also end up as a neutron star, a very compact star with the mass of several Suns and diameter of only a few miles. As mentioned above, neutron stars, also called pulsars, rotate and send out regular pulses of radiation.

Multiple Star Systems

Our star is "single," but over 50% of stars have one or more companions. The members of a star system orbit around their common center of gravity, sometimes in a very complex motion. Some star companions are very far apart. If the stars are very close, they can even exchange matter from one to the other, with the mass usually flowing from the larger star to the smaller.

How Do Astronomers Study Things So Far Away?

Waves of the spectrum: Astronomers study the color spectrum of stars using telescopes equipped with prisms or diffraction gratings. We use these colors to identify the chemical make-up of matter, even over the vast distances of space. There are other waves of the spectrum which are not visible to us, such as radio waves, microwaves and infrared. Astronomers study these too.

Looking back in time: We know that light travels at 186,000 miles per second (300,000 km/second). The light we see from a star actually left that star many years ago, so when we look at stars, we are looking back in time. The farther into space we're able to look, the farther back in time we're seeing. By looking deep into space and studying light that has traveled very far from other galaxies, astronomers can see objects and events from the very early stages of the universe, over 10 billion years ago.

Studying gravitational pull: With an understanding of gravity, astronomers can infer masses of distant objects. To figure out star masses, astronomers study stars in systems of two or more. By studying the way the stars move in relation to each other, they are able to infer the strength of their gravitational fields. Using this information, they can determine their masses. Even planets can affect stars by their gravity. Jupiter, our solar system's largest planet, pulls on our Sun so that at various times the Sun moves toward or away from us at a speed of about 3 meters per second. A heavy planet orbiting another star will also make the star shift back and forth. Astronomers can search for subtle shifts of stars, measure the shifts, and infer the masses of those planets. As should be evident, mathematics of many different kinds plays an integral role in astronomy, as well as chemistry, physics, biology, geology and earth science (including tectonic plate theory)…and lots more!

The SETI Project

What is SETI? SETI is an acronym for **S**earch for **E**xtra**T**errestrial **I**ntelligence. It is an effort to detect evidence of technological civilizations that may exist elsewhere in the universe, particularly in our galaxy. There are potentially billions of locations outside our solar system that may host life. With our current technology, we have the ability to discover evidence of cosmic habitation where life has evolved and developed to a technological level at least as advanced as our own.

How is SETI research conducted? SETI searches look for ET (extraterrestrials) by seeking signals that travel through space at the speed of light—300,000 km per second—the fastest way in the universe to communicate from one place to another. The visible light we see with our eyes when we look at the Sun and stars is only a small part of the whole energy spectrum. Gamma rays, x-rays, ultraviolet, visible, infrared, and radio comprise the entire electromagnetic spectrum and come to the Earth from everywhere in the universe. Our atmosphere blocks or absorbs most of this energy—fortunately for life on the planet. From the surface of the Earth, that means SETI searches are able to look for ET in the portions of the electromagnetic spectrum that actually reach the ground: visible (light) and radio waves.

What do SETI scientists expect to discover? The people of Earth began to broadcast signals—radio, television, radar, and microwave—less than a century ago. The same basic physics that makes broadcasting possible on Earth applies throughout the universe. SETI scientists reason that intelligent extraterrestrials will discover the same physical principals that apply here on Earth, and develop technology that takes advantage of the speed and efficiency of broadcast communications. So, researchers seek evidence of ET by looking for faint, technologically generated signals amidst the broad background noise emitted by natural processes in the universe. Most scientists expect signals from ET to be "narrowband" like our radio stations do on Earth. As you tune across the radio band, you are tuning from one narrowband signal to another. Today, scientists search for three kinds of signals: 1) carrier signals which are continuous, modulated waves like those that our TV and radio ride upon; 2) pulses which are brief, intermittent signals; and 3) chirps which are pulses whose frequency (wavelength) changes. In some ways, they are looking for the proverbial needle in a haystack because we don't know where ET lives. So there are several different strategies for

See page 141 for detailed information on the Life in the Universe curriculum of the SETI Institute.

searching for ET: general surveys of the sky, focused searches in the vicinity of nearby, Sun-like stars, and searches for interstellar beacons.

Who is doing SETI research? Scientists in many countries conduct SETI searches. Most use radio telescopes to listen for faint signals broadcast from planets in orbit about distant suns. More recently, scientists have started to conduct optical SETI searches looking in the visible portion—visible light—of the electromagnetic spectrum looking for very short (nanosecond) pulses of light which very briefly outshine the ET's own sun. The SETI Institute, a private non-profit scientific research organization, conducts Project Phoenix, a targeted star search that uses the Arecibo Observatory's giant radio dish, largest in the world, to listen for ET. Astronomers from the University of California at Berkeley are carrying out a search called SERENDIP IV at the Arecibo as well. The Planetary Society, a privately funded organization, operates Project BETA at Harvard University and in Argentina. Ohio State University has conducted a full-time search with a large volunteer effort for a couple of decades; their effort will end shortly when the university abandons the radio telescope they use. New SETI searches are being undertaken in Australia, Southern SERENDIP, and Italy. Other searches, on a smaller scale, have been, and continue to be, conducted by individual scientists and radio amateurs in the United States and other countries.

Have SETI scientists heard from ET? As of 2000, no confirmed, artificially produced extraterrestrial signal has ever been found in the 40 years of SETI searches. However, all previous searches have been limited in one respect or another. These include limits on sensitivity, frequency coverage, types of signals the equipment could detect, and the number of stars or the directions in the sky observed. For example, while there are hundreds of billions of stars in our galaxy, less than a thousand have been observed with high sensitivity. Many SETI searches have found unexplained signals, but unless a signal can be found repeatedly and confirmed by other telescopes, it won't meet the stringent requirements set by scientists for a true detection.

More Information: For up-to-date information on SETI searches, go to the SETI Institute's web site at http://www.seti.org where you will find more information, lesson plans, simulations, and live links for all of the SETI searches being conducted world-wide.

SETI Institute

Resources

Related Curriculum Material

Life in the Universe
by the SETI Institute
2035 Landings Drive
Mountain View, CA 94043
(650) 961-6633

Science Detectives (Grades 3–4)
This exciting science adventure has students trace the travels of Amelia Spacehart, as astronaut and radio astronomer who is searching the solar system for the source of a mysterious radio signal. Is it a signal from ET? From her interplanetary spacecraft, Amelia provides clues that lead students to explore feature of the solar system, states of matter, lenses and magnification, and scale modeling.

The SETI Academy Planet Project
In this three-volume set, students are invited to become members of the SETI Academy and explore the life of stars and their planets, the origin and evolution of life on Earth, and the development of humans and culture.

Evolution of a Planetary System (Grades 5–6)
Students are challenged to model and learn about stars and their planetary systems. After exploring the evolution of our solar system, students apply that information to simulate the possible evolution of a planetary system beyond our own.

How Might Life Evolve on Other Worlds? (Grades 5–6)
Students explore the evolution of life on Earth and search for clues to the evolution of life on an unknown planet beyond our solar system. Synthesizing what they learn, they design life forms that could exist on that distant planet.

The Rise of Intelligence and Culture (Grades 5–6)
Students examine concepts of intelligence, culture, technology, and communication. With this knowledge, they simulate a complex culture for an intelligent organism that could exist on an unknown planet.

Life: Here? There? Elsewhere? The Search for Life on Venus and Mars (Grades 7–9)
Students investigate the phenomena of life through activities that introduce them to the multidisciplinary sciences of planetology and exobiology. Simulating Venusian and Martian conditions, they conduct experiments using various tests for life in atmosphere and soil samples. They use their findings to propose a spacecraft design for detecting life on Venus and Mars.

Project Haystack: The Search for Life in the Galaxy (Grades 7–9)
Does ET exist? If so, where is ET and how can we communicate? Project

Haystack investigates these questions and others now being asked by scientists exploring our place in the universe. Students learn about the scale and structure of the Milky Way Galaxy—a cosmic haystack. They study SETI science by using simple astronomical tools to solve some of the problems of sending and receiving messages beyond our solar system.

For further information or to order the LITU series, please visit the SETI Institute web site at http://www.seti.org.

SETI@home

In an exciting new development, more than one million computer users around the world have been brought into the search for extraterrestrial intelligence. You and your students can join in! SETI@home is a scientific experiment based at the Space Sciences Laboratory at the University of California at Berkeley that uses Internet-connected computers in the Search for Extraterrestrial Intelligence (SETI). You can participate by running a free screensaver program that downloads and analyzes radio telescope data.

The SETI@home program is a special kind of screensaver. Like other screensavers it starts up when you leave your computer unattended, and it shuts down as soon as you return to work. While you are getting coffee, or having lunch or sleeping, your computer will be helping the Search for Extraterrestrial Intelligence by analyzing data from the Arecibo radio telescope in Puerto Rico, the largest and most sensitive radio telescope in the world.

In August of 1999, Ed Bradburn from England became the millionth SETI@home user. He wrote to the project: "The excellent film of Sagan's 'Contact' really got me interested in the concept of reaching out to search the stars (something I've been intrigued by ever since reading Asimov's 'The Gods Themselves' and Sagan and Shklovskii's 'Intelligent Life in the Universe.' I'm proud to be the 1,000,000th participant in the SETI@home project and hope that there'll be many more!"

The software can be downloaded from the SETI@home web site, which also updates the status of the search, and provides information and links on SETI, astrobiology, and astronomy. Find out more at: **http://setiathome.ssl.berkeley.edu**

Planetarium Activities for Student Success (PASS)
from the Lawrence Hall of Science
Cary Sneider, Alan Friedman and Alan Gould (Editors)

Designed for both experienced planetarium instructors and teachers using a planetarium for the first time, this series provides ready-to-go ideas and practical suggestions for planning and presenting entertaining and educationally effective programs for students. The first four books in the series provide a general orientation to astronomy and space science education, with applications for both the planetarium and classroom settings. The other eight books each present a complete planetarium program and related classroom activities. The books are 30-70 pages each, with black and white photographs and illustrations and are available for purchase individually or as a full set. These are the twelve volumes:

1. Planetarium Educator's Workshop Guide
2. Planetarium Activities for Schools
3. Resources for Teaching Astronomy & Space Science
4. A Manual for Using Portable Planetariums
5. Constellations Tonight
6. Red Planet Mars
7. Moons of the Solar System
8. Colors From Space
9. How Big Is the Universe?
10. Who "Discovered" America?
11. Astronomy of the Americas
12. Stonehenge

For more information about the PASS series, call 510-642-5863 or visit the Lawrence Hall of Science web site at http://www.lhs.berkeley.edu/pass

It's a Hands-on Universe!

Hands-On Universe™ (HOU) is a student-centered research and curriculum development program of the Lawrence Hall of Science, centered at the University of California at Berkeley. It is a collaboration between Lawrence Hall of Science, the TERC organization in Cambridge, Massachusetts, Adler Planetarium in Chicago, and Yerkes Observatory in Williams Bay, Wisconsin, as well as a network of educators and astronomers from all over the world. This exciting and innovative program enables students to investigate the Universe. Using the Internet, participants around the world request observations from an automated telescope, download images from a large image archive, and analyze them with the aid of user-friendly image processing software.

Hands-On Universe has developed and pilot tested a high school program and curriculum that integrates many of the science and mathematics topics and skills outlined in the national standards into open-ended astronomical investigations. HOU is also developing activities and tools for middle school students and products for informal science education centers. To find out more, check out the Hands-On Universe web site at: **http://hou.lbl.gov/info/**

The Mars Millennium Project

This is a youth initiative that challenges students across the nation to imagine and plan a community on the planet Mars for the year 2030. The Project is designed for formal (classroom) and informal (youth groups) educational settings. Participation kits are available for grade levels K–2, 3–5, 6–8, and 9–12, and for community organizations. Students will work on their projects during the 1999–2000 school year, project concepts will be entered into a National Registry, and finished works will be displayed in an online virtual gallery and at local and national exhibits in the spring and summer of 2000. For more information on this nationwide initiative, visit the Project web site at www.mars2030.net; e-mail mars@pvcla.com; or phone (310) 274-8787, ext. 150.

Astro Adventures: An Activity-Based Astronomy Curriculum
by Dennis Schatz and Doug Cooper
Pacific Science Center
200 Second Avenue North
Seattle, WA 98109-4895
(206) 443-2001
http://www.pacsci.org/public/education/astro/

Astro Adventures is an inventive and creative curriculum package designed to provide students with hands-on, activity-based experiences. Nineteen complete lessons and dozens of additional suggestions for exploring astronomy topics provide excitement and flexibility for teachers designing units of study about the moon, stars, planets, and sun.

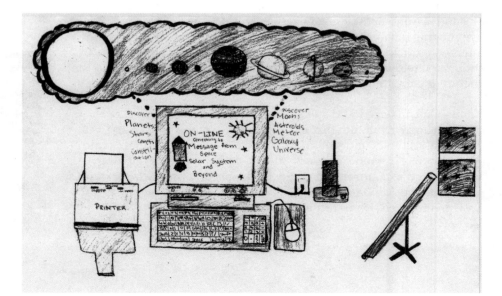

Teacher Resources

NASA, Teacher Resource Centers. To make information available to the education community, the NASA Education Division has created Teacher Resource Centers. They offer many resources for educators including publications, reference books, slide sets, audio cassettes, videotapes, telelecture programs, computer programs, lesson plans, and teacher guides with activities. A list of the centers can be found on page XX or at the NASA web site http://quest.arc.nasa.gov/space/teachers/rockets/resource_center.html.

NASA, Regional Teacher Resource Centers. NASA has formed partnerships with universities, museums, and other educational institutions to serve as RTRCs in many states. Teachers may preview, copy, or receive NASA materials at these sites. A complete list of RTRCs is available through CORE (see below).

NASA Central Operation of Resources for Educators (CORE). This was established for the national and international distribution of NASA-produced educational materials in audiovisual format. Educators can obtain a catalog of these materials and an order form by written request, on school letterhead to

> NASA CORE
> Lorain County Joint Vocational School
> 15181 Route 58 South
> Oberlin, OH 44074
> (216) 774-1051, ext. 293 or 294

Jet Propulsion Laboratory Teacher Resource Center, JPL Educational Outreach, Mail Stop CS-530, Pasadena, CA 91109; (818) 354-6916. Specializes in inquiries related to space and planetary exploration, and other JPL activities.

United States Space Foundation, 2860 South Circle Dr., Suite 2301, Colorado Springs, CO 80906-4184; (800) 691-4000. This nonprofit NASA affiliate organization promotes national awareness and support for America's space endeavors. The Foundation prepares K–12 educators in using space science and technology in the classroom to inspire students and enhance learning.

Astronomical Society of the Pacific, 390 Ashton Ave., San Francisco, CA 94112. A non-profit, international society that serves as a resource for scientists, teachers, students, and astronomy enthusiasts. Educational materials include the Astronomy Catalog of slides, software, videos, posters, and more; *The Universe In the Classroom,* a newsletter on teaching astronomy (grades 3–12); and *Mercury* magazine, the Society journal.

Association of Lunar and Planetary Observers (ALPO), c/o John E. Westfall, P.O. Box 16131, San Francisco, CA 94116. An international organization for amateur and professional astronomers. A special group of observers draw and photograph Jupiter and its moons, time special events, and watch for unusual occurrences. Teachers and students may write for information on available materials (e.g., charts, instructional handbooks, observational report forms), for the quarterly journal, or for information on workshops and conventions.

British Astronomical Association, Burlington House, Piccadilly, London, England W1V9AG. Teachers and students are invited to write this international organization of astronomers for information about this association which publishes sky charts, a journal, and educational materials for observers.

Space Telescope Science Institute, 3700 San Martin Dr., Baltimore, MD 21218. The Education and Public Affairs Office at the Space Telescope Institute offers slide sets, posters, photographs, and information packets. They sponsor teacher workshops and make available to the public a wide range of educational materials.

The Planetary Society, 65 North Catalina Ave., Pasadena, CA 91106. A non-profit organization for people interested in space exploration. Members receive *The Planetary Report,* a bimonthly magazine. Also available are an annual catalog of books, slide sets, video tapes, models, computer software, posters, T-shirts, and gifts.

Recommended Reading

(Many of these references and reviews were provided by the Astronomical Society of the Pacific, Teachers Resource Notebook, a bibliography on the SETI Institute web site, and SETI's Life in the Universe curriculum series.)

Reference Books

Exploring the Night Sky with Binoculars, Patrick Moore, Cambridge University Press, New York, 1986.
    Clear and simple introduction to the subject.

A Field Guide to the Stars and Planets, D. Menzel and J. Pasachoff, Houghton Mifflin, Boston, 1983.
    Updated edition of a classic guide full of information and maps.

The Kingfisher Young People's Book of Space, Martin Redfern, Kingfisher, New York, 1998.
    Examines our exploration of outer space and discusses the solar system, stars, galaxies, and the universe in general.

Magnificent Universe, Ken Crosswell, Simon & Schuster, New York, 1999
Beautiful collection of the most up-to-date images from the Hubble space telescope, observatories worldwide, and interplanetary spacecraft.

The New Solar System, J. Kelly Beatty, Brian O'Leary, and Andrew Chaikin, eds., Sky Publishing, Cambridge, New York, 1990.
Beautifully illustrated with articles on all aspects of planetary astronomy.

Observer's Handbook, R. Bishop, ed. Royal Astronomical Society of Canada, 136 Dupont St., Toronto, Ontario M5R 1V2.
An annual guide to celestial events and cycles.

To the Edge of the Universe, The Exploration of Outer Space with NASA, Bill Yenne and S. Garratte, ed., Exeter Books, distributed by Bookthrift Marketing, New York, 1986.
What we have learned since astronomy began and mysteries that remain to be solved.

Whitney's Star Finder: A Field Guide to the Heavens, Charles A. Whitney, Knopf, New York, 1990.
Basic primer on constellations and sky phenomena. (Updated periodically.)

For Students (and Teachers, too!)

After Contact: The Human Response to Extraterrestrial Life, Albert A. Harrison, Plenum Publishing, New York, 1997.
The book addresses how we will respond to extraterrestrial life forms and asserts that psychological, sociological, political, and cultural factors are integral to the search for intelligent life forms from other worlds.

Amazing Spacefacts: Solar System-Stars-Space Travel, Susan Goodman, Peter Bedrick Books, New York, 1993.
Lists many facts and uses excellent full-color photographs and illustrations.

Barlowe's Guide to Extraterrestrials: Great Aliens from Science Fiction Literature, Wayne Douglas Barlowe, Workman Publishing, New York, 1979.
A classic guide to extraterrestrials with full-color illustrations of 50 aliens from popular science fiction literature.

Before the Sun Dies: The Story of Evolution, Roy Gallant, Macmillan, New York, 1989.
A complete, well-written book on the evolution of our solar system, Earth, and life.

The Biological Universe: The Twentieth-Century Extraterrestrial Life Debate and the Limits of Science, Steven J. Dick, Cambridge University Press, New York, 1996.

Provides a well-researched account of our century's attempts to discover extraterrestrial life, from UFO sightings and Martian "canals" to the *Viking* mission and SETI.

Colonizing the Planets and Stars, Isaac Asimov, 1990.

Explores the possibility of establishing colonies in space, traveling by starship to other galaxies, and meeting extraterrestrials. NASA photos and color illustrations.

Cosmos, Carl Sagan, Random House, New York, 1980.

Based on the award-winning PBS-TV series, this bestseller offers an introduction to astronomical knowledge from one of the sharpest minds in science. Chapter 12 explores the central concepts of the SETI endeavor.

First Contact: The Search for Extraterrestrial Intelligence, Ben Bova and Byron Preiss, editors, New American Library Books, New York, 1990.

The Golden Book of Stars and Planets, Judith Herbst, Western Publishing Co., Inc., Racine, Wisconsin, 1988.

Basic introduction to the origins of astronomy, the solar system, descriptions of planets' sizes, atmospheres, environments, plus comets, meteors, etc. NASA photos and color illustrations.

The History and Practice of Ancient Astronomy, by James Evans, Oxford University Press, New York, 1998.

Carefully organized and generously illustrated, the book can teach readers how to do real astronomy using the methods of ancient astronomers.

Is Anybody Out There? The Search for Life Beyond Our Planet, Heather Couper and Nigel Henbest, DK Publishing, New York, 1998.

In this book readers can decipher the codes and messages sent into space, examine recent data from astronomers, and judge for themselves whether or not intelligent life could exist beyond our planet. The book also has a wide array of illustrations of what other life forms might look like.

Is Anyone Out There? The Scientific Search for Extraterrestrial Intelligence, Frank Drake and D. Sobel, Delacorte Press, New York, 1992.

The astronomer who pioneered the radio search for extraterrestrial civilizations provides a personal view of the SETI saga.

Meteors and Meteorites—Voyagers from Space, Patricia Lauber, Thomas Y. Crowell Jr. Books, New York, 1989.

Explores current scientific thinking about meteorites as clues to the origin of the solar system, and about violent collisions with comets and space rocks. NASA photos, pictures, and drawings.

The Natural History of the Universe: From the Big Bang to the End of Time, Colin A. Ronan, Macmillan, New York, 1991.

Contains thorough descriptions of the planets and other heavenly bodies, plus a vast amount of information on the creation of the universe and on the building blocks and conditions necessary for life.

Other Worlds: Is There Life Out There?, David Darling, Dillon Press, Minneapolis, Minnesota, 1985.

Answers common questions and describes the search for life on other planets. Gives evidence that suggests the possibility of life in other stellar systems and the means by which we might detect it. The book is part of the Discovering Our Universe series.

The Planet Hunters: The Search for Other Worlds, Dennis B. Fradin, McElderry Books, New York, 1997.

Provides historical information on astronomy, the discovery of the planets, and the people who have made such discoveries.

The Planets—The Next Frontier, David J. Darling, Dillon Press, Minneapolis, Minnesota, 1985.

Describes our solar system, and what we know of each planet from spacecraft. Includes Voyager's discoveries in the systems of Jupiter and Saturn. Color illustrations.

Powers of Ten, Philip and Phylis Morrison, W.H. Freeman, New York, 1982.

Forty two different views of the same picnic are shown— each one a power of ten different from the view it borders. The views begin from about 1 billion light years away from Earth, travel through our familiar daily scale, then go on to the microscopic. A great help to learn about scale. See also the video, listed below.

The Quest for Alien Planets: Exploring Worlds Outside the Solar System, Paul Halpern, Plenum Publishing, New York, 1997.

An accessible account of the recent findings of the search for worlds outside our solar system. The book answers such questions as "Are we alone in the cosmos?" and "Are there other planets like Earth in the Universe?" and guides readers on an exciting journey to nearby stars and their planetary companions.

The Science of Aliens, Clifford A. Pickover, HarperCollins, New York, 1998.

An intriguing book featuring chapters such as "What Aliens Look Like," "Origin of Alien Life," "Alien Senses," and "Communication." The book contains mathematical "alien messages" to decipher.

The Search for Extraterrestrial Intelligence: Listening for Life in the Cosmos, Thomas R. McDonough, Wiley, New York, 1987.

After examining humanity's long fascination with the possibility of life in other parts of the universe, SETI scientist McDonough turns his attention to today's radio astronomical investigations that may reveal the presence of other civilizations.

The Search for Extraterrestrial Life, William A. Gutsch, Crown Publishers, New York, 1991.

Discusses serious attempts by astronomers to contact intelligent alien civilizations and detect signals sent out by them.

Seeing Earth from Space, Patricia Lauber, Orchard Books, New York, 1990.

Beautiful and intriguing photographs of spaceship Earth. Focuses on what can be learned by studying images formed from data collected by satellites.

Sharing the Universe: Perspectives on Extraterrestrial Life, Seth Shostak, Berkeley Hills Books, Berkeley, California, 1998.

A highly recommended, popular, and up-to-date account of the search for extraterrestrials, their likely construction and behavior. The book includes a fascinating and well-written discussion of how the SETI movement began and the history of the SETI Institute. There is also a very accessible discussion of the origins and significance of the Drake Equation. The author helped to review this teacher's guide.

Space Library: Space Walking, Gregory Vogt, Franklin Watts, New York, 1987.

A description of human beings' ability to survive in space. Explains space suits, space and moonwalks, space stations, and future projects in space. NASA photos of space walks in space and on the Moon.

Visions of the Universe, paintings by Kazuaki Iwasaki, text by Isaac Asimov, preface by Carl Sagan, The Cosmos Store, a division of Carl Sagan Productions, Montrose, California, 1981.

From the Sun, through all nine planets, several moons, and other celestial bodies, the paintings in this book provide an accurate image of many elements of our solar system. Several of the paintings offer a unique perspective—such as a view of Saturn from Rhea, one of its satellites. Each painting is accompanied by clear, simple, and informative text.

Voyager, Missions in Space, Gregory Vogt, Millbrook Press, Brookfield, Connecticut, 1991.

An "inside look" at the missions of Voyager 1 and 2. Includes beautiful NASA images of the Gas Giants, their satellites, and deep space.

Magazines and Newsletters

Abrams Planetarium Sky Calendar. Available free with membership in the Astronomical Society of the Pacific (see "Teacher Resources" above) or from Abrams Planetarium, Michigan State University, East Lansing, MI 48824. Concise one-page monthly sky calendar and simple star chart tells you what to look for and where each month.

Astronomy. Kalmbach Publishing, P.O. Box 1612, Waukesha, WI 53187. Monthly magazine for beginners and other astronomy enthusiasts.

Astronomy Day Handbook. Published by The Astronomical League for organizations wishing to plan special Astronomy Day events. Includes ideas for special events and activities, and gives over 200 addresses for astronomical organizations and sources for educational materials, including space camps, scholarships, teacher training courses, and publications for classroom teachers. Contact Gary Tomlinson, Astronomy Day Coordinator, Public Museum of Grand Rapids, 54 Jefferson S.E., Grand Rapids, MI 49503; (616) 456-3987.

Education Horizons, NASA, Educational Publications Services, XEP, Washington, DC 20546. This is a free newsletter full of the latest NASA information, research, and educational resource materials for teachers.

Odyssey. Cobblestone Publishing, Inc., 30 Grove St., Peterborough, NH 03458; (603) 924-7209. Monthly magazine that includes basic astronomy, word games, and puzzles for young astronomers. (Ages 8–14; published 10 times per year.)

Sky & Telescope. Sky Publishing, P.O. Box 9111, Belmont, MA 02178. Monthly magazine with articles written by and for the professional and amateur astronomer.

STARnews. Project STAR, Center for Astrophysics, 60 Garden St., Cambridge, MA 02138. A quarterly newsletter specializing in teaching astronomy at the secondary level.

The Universe In the Classroom: A Newsletter on Teaching Astronomy. Astronomical Society of the Pacific, Teacher's Newsletter, Dept. N, 390 Ashton Ave., San Francisco, CA 94112. A free classroom resource for grades 3–12. (Please write on *school stationary* and indicate grade level to be included on the mailing list.)

Videos

Contact, Warner Home Video, 162 mins., 1998.
  Astronomer Dr. Ellie Arroway (Jodi Foster) receives an encrypted message, apparently from a solar system many light years away. Based on the novel by Carl Sagan (see "Literature Connections").

Contact: The Search for Extraterrestrial Intelligence, Space Viz Productions, 48 mins., 1995.
  A thought-provoking exploration that asks important questions about where we came from, where we're going, and whether or not we're going there alone. Contains interviews with leading astronomers and cosmologists, and offers a well-balanced overview of the subject.

The Creation of the Universe, PBS Home Video, 92 mins., 1985.
  Using spectacular special effects, animation, computer graphics, and interviews with internationally renowned physicists, this program explores clues to the origin and evolution of the entire universe.

Powers of Ten, Pyramid Film & Video, 21 mins., 1978.
  Presents a visual size continuum from galaxies to atomic nuclei—by steps that are a power of 10 from one another. Helps in understanding the large numbers and distances involved in the solar system. Also available from PBS Home Video (800-645-4PBS) or Arbor Scientific (800-367-6695). See also the book by the same title, listed above.

Reading Rainbow, Lancit Media, GPN (Great Plains National), 30 mins., 1986.
  In the "Space Case" episode, the question "What would it be like to meet beings from another planet?" is explored. Host LeVar Burton takes a field trip to the Lick Observatory and to the site of a radio telescope at Arecibo, Puerto Rico.

The Solar System, Allied Film and Video, 20 mins., 1978.

Through the animation and NASA footage in this video, students take a voyage through space, view the origins of the solar system, and learn the geologic makeup of each planet.

A Few Movie Reviews

The film *Contact* is an excellent complement to this unit. Based on the book of the same name by Carl Sagan, it is available on video. The lead character is loosely based on Dr. Jill Tarter of the SETI Institute. In a brief special effects sequence at the start of the film the camera travels from Earth out through and beyond the solar system. A melange of radio messages (current to 1997) is heard. As the camera moves away, the radio messages are from further and further in the past. It flies past the moon, then Mars, through the asteroid belt, past Jupiter, then leaves the solar system. With extreme distance, Earth's radio signals become sparse, then go silent. Eventually the camera leaves the Milky Way galaxy, and flies through a few other galaxies. The sequence ends flying past thousands of galaxies, so many that they become a blur. This is a great tour of the solar system and beyond, depicting the incomprehensible number of stars. It is also a nice introduction to the idea that (1) radio waves can travel through vast space, and (2) the longer ago radio waves were sent out, the farther from Earth they are now. (One unfortunate inaccuracy in the film is the use of radio sounds from the 1950s as the camera travels past Jupiter—in reality radio waves can travel through our solar system in a matter of hours. So radio signals from the 1950s, and earlier, are now far beyond the solar system—way out in space!) If you have time you might also consider showing other excerpts from *Contact,* such as images of Arecibo (the huge radio telescope in Puerto Rico) or the VLA (Very Large Array, a large group of smaller radio telescopes in New Mexico). You could also include the lead character's quote on the probability of life on other planets, and the exciting scenes and surprises when the scientists receive a pictorial and mathematical message and struggle to interpret it. You may want to skip the second half of the film, which moves into more philosophical and imaginary realms of "traveling" through space to those who sent the message. The film is rated PG for what is described as "some intense action, mild language and a scene of sensuality."

The film *Men in Black* also includes a special effects tour through space at the end of the film. This tour is much faster (and harder to follow) than the sequence in *Contact,* and concludes with a whimsical scene of an alien playing marbles—with our entire galaxy inside one of the marbles! This film is rated PG 13. The film *Independence Day* includes a scene toward the beginning of a

For more information on the life and work of Dr. Jill Tarter of the SETI Institute, have your students do an Internet search and you'll find lots of interesting stories and interviews. For example, in a "live chat" with ABCNews.com, Dr. Tarter is quoted as saying, "I'd grown up with Saturday morning cartoons—Buck Rogers and Flash Gordon and that sort of thing and I guess there was never a time when I didn't just absolutely assume that the stars in the sky were somebody else's suns." She also commented on the film Contact, saying, "I thought Contact was a superb movie—the first time scientists were portrayed as we are—not some crazies in white lab coats about to blow up or save the world..."

message being received from outer space by a SETI search. This film quickly moves into a more fantastic (and stereotypical) realm, when it turns out that the message is coming from an ET's spacecraft about to attack Earth. This film is rated PG13.

CD-ROMS

Starry Night

Starry Night is an outstanding computer software program that allows you and your students to virtually navigate the Universe! One of the leading "desktop planetarium" programs, it has received rave reviews from many sources for its ease of use, beautiful graphics, and seamless design. *New Scientist* magazine said, "Starry Night is effortless astronomy software that lets you go anywhere in the Solar System. Watch an eclipse from a planet, its moon, and the Sun, all at the same time." *Popular Science* said, "Starry Night is the closest you can come to space travel without a heavy suit and a lot of training." *Sky and Telescope* called it an "amazing sky simulator." Three versions of Starry Night are available from Sienna Software. The web site provides detailed information on all three versions at http://www.siennasoft.com

Sienna Software, Inc.
411 Richmond Street East, Suite 303
Toronto Ontario,
Canada, M5A 3S5
(416) 410-0259 (phone)
(800) 252-5417 (orders)

The Great Solar System Rescue   Grades 5–8

This excellent laserdisc package (also available on CD-ROM) is designed to engage students in learning about the solar system and other aspects of planetary science. It contains a cooperative learning Rescue Activity and a Video Library filled with movies and stills. The Rescue Activity involves students in four missions to rescue probes lost in the solar system. Nineteen associated lesson plans involve students in experiments, simulations, investigations, and other activities that further explore the content area.

Tom Snyder Productions, Inc.
80 Coolidge Hill Road
Watertown, Massachusetts 02172-2817
Toll-free: (800) 342-0236
Note: Can be ordered on 45-day trial basis.

Internet Sites

- A large collection of Astronomy related URLs
  http://www.lhs.berkeley.edu/sii/URLs/URLs-Astronomy.html

- The SETI Institute
  http://www.seti.org

- SETI@home
  http://setiathome.ssl.berkeley.edu

- NASA Educational Resources
  http://education.nasa.gov/
  http://nssdc.gsfc.nasa.gov/planetary/planetfact.html

- Goddard Space Flight Center Space Science Education Home Page
  http://www.gsfc.nasa.gov/education/education_home.html

- Remote Sensing Public Access Center
  http://www.rspac.ivv.nasa.gov

- Hubble Space Telescope and Amazing Space (web-based educational activities)
  http://www.stsci.edu/public.html

- Astronomical Society of the Pacific
  http://www.aspsky.org

- The Nine Planets
  http://www.seds.org/billa/tnp/nineplanets.html

- The Nine Planets for Kids
  http://www.tcsn.net/afiner/

- PlanetScapes
  http://planetscapes.com/

- Solar System Model
  http://www.bradley.edu/las/phy/solar_system.html

- Earth-Moon System to Scale
  http://www.dnr.state.oh.us/odnr/geo_survey/edu/hands10.htm

- Global Quest: The Internet in the Classroom
  http://quest.arc.nasa.gov

- Smithsonian Institute "Museum Without Walls"
  http://www.si.edu

- Exploratorium (scale model)
  http://www.exploratorium.edu/ronh/solar_system/

- Views of the Solar System
  http://spaceart.com/solar/

There are so many wonderful astronomy-related sites on the world wide web. These are only a few!

How to Make Your Own Radiometer

Please note: Any students constructing a radiometer should work under the supervision of an adult.

How does the radiometer work? The darkened foil absorbs heat while the shiny foil reflects it. The difference in temperature causes the blades to rotate.

What You Need

For each radiometer:

- ❏ a sheet of tin foil
- ❏ a large jar (glass or clear plastic)
- ❏ 1 round toothpick
- ❏ a candle
- ❏ matches
- ❏ about 10" of string
- ❏ scissors
- ❏ a pencil
- ❏ glue

1. From the sheet of foil, cut two 2" x 1/2" strips. Bend each strip 1" from the short end to form an "L" shape.

2. Glue the outer edge of the fold in each strip to the center of the round toothpick. Let dry.

3. Light the candle and use the flame to darken four faces of the tin on the toothpick. The four faces to be darkened are shown in the illustration. Hold one end of the toothpick and carefully move the tin close to the flame. Allow the soot to darken the appropriate faces of the tin.

4. Glue one end of the string to the toothpick/tin apparatus. Allow the glue to dry.

5. Balance the pencil across the top of the open jar. Hold the string and lower the toothpick/tin apparatus into the jar. Tie the free end of the string to the pencil, adjusting it to allow the apparatus to hang suspended from the pencil without touching the bottom of the jar. Trim excess string as necessary.

6. Test the finished radiometer by placing it near a bare light bulb or in a sunny window. If it doesn't spin well, check that the toothpick is not touching the bottom of the jar or that the string hangs easily from the pencil. You may need to make the four faces of tin darker with soot.

NASA Teacher Resource Center Network

If you live in:	Center Education Program Officer	Teacher Resource Center
Alaska Arizona California Hawaii Idaho Montana Nevada Oregon Utah Washington Wyoming	Mr. Garth A. Hull Chief, Education Programs Branch Mail Stop 204-12 **NASA Ames Research Center** Moffett Field, CA 94035-1000 (415) 604-5543	NASA Teacher Resource Center Mail Stop T12-A **NASA Ames** **Research Center** Moffett Field, CA 94035-1000 (415) 604-3574
Connecticut Delaware District of Columbia Maine Maryland Massachusetts New Hampshire New Jersey New York Pennsylvania Rhode Island Vermont	Educational Programs Code 130 **NASA Goddard Space** **Flight Center** Greenbelt, MD 20771-0001 (301) 286-7206	NASA Teacher Resource Laboratory Mail Code 130.3 **NASA Goddard Space** **Flight Center** Greenbelt, MD 20771-0001 (301) 286-8570
Colorado Kansas Nebraska New Mexico North Dakota Oklahoma South Dakota Texas	Dr. Robert W. Fitzmaurice Center Education Program Officer Education & Information Services Branch - AP2 2101 NASA Road 1 **NASA Johnson Space Center** Houston, TX 77058-3696 (713) 483-1257	NASA Teacher Resource Room Mail Code AP2 2101 NASA Road 1 **NASA Johnson Space Center** Houston, TX 77058-3696 (713) 483-8696
Florida Georgia Puerto Rico Virgin Islands	Dr. Steve Dutczak Chief, Education Services Branch Mail Code PA-ESB **NASA Kennedy Space Center** Kennedy Space Center, FL 32899-0001 (407) 867-4444	NASA Educators Resource Laboratory Mail Code ERL **NASA Kennedy Space Center** Kennedy Space Center, FL 32899-0001 (407) 867-4090
Kentucky North Carolina South Carolina Virginia West Virginia	Ms. Marchelle Canright Center Education Program Officer Mail Stop 400 **NASA Langley** **Research Center** Hampton, VA 23681-0001 (804) 864-3313	NASA Teacher Resource Center for **NASA Langley** **Research Center** Virginia Air and Space Center 600 Settler's Landing Road Hampton, VA 23699-4033 (804)727-0900 x757

Illinois Indiana Michigan Minnesota Ohio Wisconsin	Ms. Jo Ann Charleston Acting Chief, Office of Educational Programs Mail Stop 7-4 **NASA Lewis Research Center** 21000 Brookpark Road Cleveland, OH 44135-3191 (216) 433-2957	NASA Teacher Resource Center Mail Stop 8-1 **NASA Lewis Research Center** 21000 Brookpark Road Cleveland, OH 44135-3191 (216) 433-2017
Alabama Arkansas Iowa Louisiana Missouri Tennessee	Mr. Jim Pruitt Acting Director, Education Programs Office Mail Stop CL 01 **NASA Marshall Space Flight Center** Huntsville, AL 35812-0001 (205) 544-8800	NASA Teacher Resource Center for **NASA Marshall Space Flight Center** U.S. Space and Rocket Center P.O. Box 070015 Huntsville, AL 35807-7015 (205) 544-5812
Mississippi	Dr. David Powe Manager, Educational Programs Mail Stop MA00 **NASA John C. Stennis Space Center** Stennis Space Center, MS 39529-6000 (601) 688-1107	NASA Teacher Resource Center Building 1200 **NASA John C. Stennis Space Center** Stennis Space Center, MS 39529-6000 (601) 688-3338
The Jet Propulsion Laboratory (JPL) serves inquiries related to space and planetary exploration and other JPL activities.	Dr. Fredrick Shair Manager, Educational Affairs Office Mail Code 183-900 **NASA Jet Propulsion Laboratory** 4800 Oak Grove Drive Pasadena, CA 91109-8099 (818) 354-8251	NASA Teacher Resource Center JPL Educational Outreach Mail Stop CS-530 **NASA Jet Propulsion Laboratory** 4800 Oak Grove Drive Pasadena, CA 91109-8099 (818) 354-6916
California (mainly cities near Dryden Flight Research Facility)		NASA Teacher Resource Center Public Affairs Office (Trl. 42) **NASA Dryden Flight Research Facility** Edwards, CA 93523-0273 (805) 258-3456
Virginia and Maryland's eastern shores	NASA Teacher Resource Lab	NASA Goddard Space Flight Center **Wallops Flight Facility** Education Complex - Visitor Center Building J-17 Wallops Island, VA 23337-5099 (804) 824-2297/2298

Assessment Suggestions

Selected Student Outcomes

1. Students increase their knowledge of the planets, moons, and other bodies in the solar system, and of how the solar system may have formed.

2. Students are able to consider and compare the different types of stars, their lifespans and lifezones.

3. Students are able to summarize what scientists believe to be the main conditions necessary for life, as we know it, to evolve.

4. Students are able to bring improved critical and scientific thinking skills to bear on reports about extraterrestrial life and "messages from space" and are able to analyze the possibility of life on other planets orally and in writing.

5. Students gain enhanced mathematical and conceptual understanding of the vast distances involved in space, and improve their ability to comprehend the scale and relative proportions involved in the solar system and beyond.

Built-In (Embedded) Assessments

Initial Ideas. Activity 1, Session 1, opens with a discussion about what students have heard about extraterrestrials and the kinds of signals that might be sent. Student comments and responses to the four messages can provide an initial sense of students' ideas about extraterrestrials. (Outcome 4)

Decoding the Message. Student work on the message can provide insight into analytic and independent thinking skills, as well as indicate early levels of understanding of the images of a different star system and other astronomical phenomena. Work on the message during the unit can also demonstrate perseverance, an essential element of good scientific work. (Outcomes 2, 4)

Star Types and Lifezones. The Lifezones discussion in Activity 2 can provide information on initial student understandings of the conditions considered necessary for life. Later, when students design their own planetary system and write stories about it, the teacher can evaluate their understanding of both start lifezones and lifespans. (Outcomes 2, 4)

From A Swirling Cloud. Two discussions in Activity 3 provide insight into initial student ideas about current theories of solar system formation. Before the water and pepper activity, students are challenged to come up with their own explanations. During the activity, they discuss how their observations may relate to how the solar system formed. Later in the unit, teachers can see whether or not students raise this idea in discussions, consider how the distant planetary system in the message from space may have formed, or include related information in their science fiction stories. (Outcome 1)

Assessment Suggestions *(continued)*

Solar System Travel Brochure. The travel brochure and tour provide teachers with a rich assessment opportunity. In addition to indicating the knowledge students have gained and their ability to communicate it to others, teachers can assess how effective students are in presenting information in an interesting, educational manner. Teachers may also want to evaluate how well students communicate big ideas and key facts, not just smaller details. Teachers can add their own assessment criteria, informing students beforehand about how their work will be evaluated. (Outcomes 1, 5)

Devising Distant Planetary Systems. In Activity 5, students design a planetary system where the message may have originated. This provides the teacher with an excellent way to assess how well students are able to bring together much of the content in the unit, as well as gain insight into students' creative and independent thinking abilities. (Outcomes 1, 2, 3, 4)

Science Fiction Stories. In Activity 6, students write science fiction stories. With the emphasis in the stories on scientific accuracy, and on providing cogent explanations for whatever strange events or lifeforms are described, the stories also provide a fertile field for assessment of how well students can apply information gained in the unit in this new creative context. See also the specific suggestions for assessment in Activity 6. (Outcomes 1, 2, 4)

Additional Assessment Ideas

Solar System Jeopardy. Devise a Jeopardy-type question-driven game for the class to test their knowledge about the planets and other aspects of the solar system they've been exposed to through the Fact Sheets and other resources. (Outcome 1)

Critical Reading Assignment. The reading assignment that follows Activity 5, and especially the class discussion of the articles, provides information on critical thinking skills, and the ability to distinguish a scientifically-based article from a more sensationalist one. (Outcome 4)

The Drake Equation. This intriguing exercise, originated by Frank Drake, the scientist who founded SETI, has strong mathematics content. From student estimates teachers can also gain a sense of students' understanding of the probability that life exists elsewhere in the Universe. (Outcomes 1, 2, 3, 4)

Your Galactic Address. Student work on this "Going Further" activity can provide a sense of how well students are able to locate themselves, from their seat in the classroom to the Milky Way Galaxy. (Outcome 5)

Dialogue Between an Earthling and an Extraterrestrial. You may want to give students a dialogue-writing assignment, asking them to compare and contrast physical features and conditions necessary for survival for humans and an imaginary extraterrestrial. (Outcomes 3, 4)

Literature Connections

2010: Odyssey Two
by Arthur C. Clarke
Ballantine Books, New York. 1982   Grades: 10–Adult

This complex, mysterious, and thought-provoking sequel to Clarke's *2001: A Space Odyssey* had the benefit of being written subsequent to the Voyager mission. There are fascinating observations, accurate scientific information, and lots of interesting speculation about Jupiter and its moons throughout the book, not to mention spirits of intergalactic intelligence and Jupiter becoming a second sun.

Against Infinity
by Gregory Benford
Simon & Schuster, New York. 1983   Grades: 10–Adult

This science fiction novel is an account of human settlement on Jupiter's largest moon, Ganymede. The story takes place several hundred years into the colonization process, and begins from the perspective of a 13-year-old boy whose father is one of the leaders of the settlement. The author is a Professor of Physics at the University of California, Irvine.

Alan Mendelsohn, The Boy from Mars
by Daniel M. Pinkwater
Dutton, New York. 1979   Grades: 5–8

Leonard's life at his new junior high is just barely tolerable until he becomes friends with the unusual Alan and shares an extraordinary adventure with him.

Contact: A Novel
by Carl Sagan
Simon & Schuster, New York. 1985   Grades: 7–Adult

When a message from outer space is detected by a worldwide system of radio telescopes, astrophysicist Ellie Arroway decodes it and builds the machine for which the message gave instructions. Then she and others of a small multinational team board the machine and take an amazing trip to outer space for the most awesome encounter in human history. Has been made into a movie of the same name.

The Drop in My Drink: The Story of Water on Our Planet
by Meredith Hooper; illustrated by Chris Coady
Viking Press, New York. 1998   Grades: 6–9

Here is the amazing and ever-changing story of water—where it comes from, how it behaves, why it matters—and the crucial role it has played throughout life on Earth. The eye-catching illustrations are realistic and thought-provoking.

Einstein Anderson Lights Up the Sky
by Seymour Simon; illustrated by Fred Winkowski
Viking Press, New York. 1982   Grades: 4–7

In Chapter 2, "The World in His Hands," Einstein punctures his friend Stanley's plan to build a scale model of the solar system in his basement. He discusses the relative sizes of the Sun and the planets and the distances between them. In Chapter 5, "The Stars Like Grains of Sand," Einstein enlightens his younger brother Dennis about the star population.

Einstein Anderson Makes Up for Lost Time
by Seymour Simon; illustrated by Fred Winkowski
Viking Penguin, New York. 1981   Grades: 4–7

Chapter 6 poses the question "How can Einstein tell a planet from a star without using a telescope?" He explains to his friend Dennis that although stars twinkle, planets usually shine with a steady light. Looking through the telescope, he thinks the steady light he sees is Jupiter. The four faint points of steady light nearby are Jupiter's moons.

Einstein Anderson Tells a Comet's Tale
by Seymour Simon; illustrated by Fred Winkowski
Viking Press, New York. 1981   Grades: 4–7

Chapter 1, "Tale of the Comet" provides some very interesting information about possible connections between comets, asteroids, and dinosaurs.

The Faces of CETI
by Mary Caraker
Houghton Mifflin, Boston. 1991   Grades: 6–12

In this science fiction thriller, colonists from Earth form two settlements on adjoining planets of the Tau Ceti system. One colony tries to survive by dominating the natural forces that they encounter, while those on the planet Ceti apply sound ecological principles and strive to live harmoniously in their new environment. Nonetheless, the Cetians encounter a terrible dilemma—

the only edible food appears to be a species of native animals called the Hlur. Two teen-age colonists risk their lives to save their fellow colonists from starvation without killing the gentle Hlur.

In the Beginning: Creation Stories from Around the World
by Virginia Hamilton; illustrated by Barry Moser
Harcourt Brace Jovanovich, San Diego. 1988   Grades: All

An illustrated collection of twenty-five legends that explain the creation of the world, with commentary placing the myth geographically and by type of myth tradition. Some of the selections are extracted from larger works such as *Popol Vuh* or the Icelandic Eddas. Makes a great connection to Activity 3's activity on formation of the solar system.

The Jupiter Theft
by Donald Moffitt
Ballantine Books, New York. 1977   Grades: 7–Adult

Strange, advanced beings from somewhere near the constellation of Cygnus encounter a Jupiter expedition from Earth. The Cygnans want to take Jupiter away to use as a power source as they migrate through the universe. There is some violence as various life forms attack and/or ally with each other, but the general focus is on scientific speculation about the possibilities and varieties of life on other worlds.

Planet of Exile
by Ursula LeGuin
Ace Books, New York. 1966   Grades: 6–Adult

Cooperation is the central theme of this book about the clash of three cultures—two that have inhabited this harsh planet for eons, and one that has been exiled only a few generations. Difficult seasonal conditions on the planet are the result of how long it takes for the planet to revolve once around its central star. Because one "year" is equivalent to many Earth years, people only live through a very small number of winters.

The Planet of Junior Brown
by Virginia Hamilton
Macmillan Publishing, New York. 1971   Grades: 8–12

This moving book begins with two African-American students—who often cut 8th grade classes—and a school custodian—who was formerly a teacher—meeting in a secret room in a school basement with a working model of the solar system. The model has one incredible addition—a giant planet named for one of the students, Junior Brown. How can the Earth's orbit not be affected by this giant planet? Is there a belt of asteroids that balances it all out? How does this relate to equilateral triangles? From these subjects, the book expands outward into the Manhattan streets and inward into the hearts, minds, and friendship of the students. After the first chapter, the solar system becomes more metaphor than model, until the end of the book when the real model must be dismantled and the three must find a way to help Junior Brown. Powerfully and poetically written, this book has also been made into a film.

The Planets
edited by Byron Preiss
Bantam Books, New York. 1985   Grades: 8–Adult

This extremely rich, high-quality anthology pairs a non-fiction essay with a fictional work about the Earth, Moon, each of the planets, and asteroids and comets. Introductory essays are by Issac Asimov, Arthur C. Clarke, and others. The material is dazzlingly illustrated with color photographs from NASA and the Jet Propulsion Laboratory, and paintings by artists such as the movie production designers of *2001* and *Star Wars*.

Space Songs
by Myra Cohn Livingston; illustrated by Leonard E. Fisher
Holiday House, New York. 1988   Grades: 5–12

Series of short poems about aspects of outer space including the Milky Way, Moon, Sun, stars, planets, comets, meteorites, asteroids, and satellites. Although the astronomy content is limited, it is accurate. The black background illustrations are dynamic and involving.

Star Tales: North American Indian Stories
retold and illustrated by Gretchen W. Mayo
Walker & Co., New York. 1987   Grades: 5–12

The nine legends in this collection explain observations of the stars, Moon, and night sky. Accompanying each tale is information about the constellation or other heavenly observation and how various peoples perceived it.

Stinker from Space
by Pamela F. Service
Charles Scribner's Sons, New York. 1988
Ballantine Books, New York. 1989   Grades: 5–8

A girl encounters an extraterrestrial being who has had to inhabit the body of a skunk after an emergency landing. The girl and a neighbor boy help the skunk, Tsynq Yr (Stinker), to evade his enemies, the Zarnks, and get an important message to his own people. Stinker's departure from Earth involves "borrowing" the space shuttle.

They Dance in the Sky: Native American Star Myths
by Jean Guard Monroe and Ray A. Williamson
Houghton Mifflin, Boston. 1987   Grades: 2–8

This book, which is great for reading aloud, includes stories from many Native American regions and peoples. Stories about the Pleiades, the Big Dipper, and the "Star Beings" are particularly noteworthy, but all are imaginative and intriguing. Stories like these from Native American and other world cultures can be interwoven with astronomy activities, provide a sense of careful observation over time, and highlight how the stars and planets have always inspired the human imagination.

To Space and Back
by Sally Ride with Susan Okie
Lothrop, Lee and Shepard/Morrow, New York. 1986
Grades: 4–7

This is a fascinating description of what it is like to travel in space—to live, sleep, eat, and work in conditions unlike anything we know on Earth, complete with colored photographs aboard ship and in space. The astronauts conducted a number of scientific experiments as they observed and photographed the stars, the Earth, the planets, and galaxies. Working outside the shuttle, they feel the warmth of the Sun through their gloves, but cool off on the dark side of Earth in the shade.

The Worst Band in the Universe: A Totally Cosmic Musical Adventure (with CD)
by Graeme Base
Harry N. Abrams, Inc., New York. 1999   Grades: 4–9

This wonderfully illustrated, poetic, and highly amusing book/ recording takes place in a distant planetary system. Accused of the crime of "musical innovation" 13-year-old Sprocc, a Splingtwanger-player, departs Blipp, his home planet. He is tricked into entering a Worst Band contest that strands him on remote Wastedump B19, then helps build a music-driven spaceship, which gets him back to Blipp in time for a high-volume, onstage face-off with the power-mad Musical Inquisitor. Complete with a CD of music composed and performed by Base himself, this whimsical science fiction journey is a true marvel.

Summary Outlines

Activity 1: Message From Space

Getting Ready

1. Copy A Binary Message for each student.

2. If you can, make tape recording of the four sounds.

3. If no tape, practice making the signals yourself.

4. If you've decided to show a video clip, set up the VCR.

Session 1: Making Contact

What Are We Looking For?

1. Ask students if they know any stories about messages from outer space or extraterrestrials. These stories come from authors who are human beings.

2. Explain that in the early 1980s some scientists began a project called SETI, which stands for **S**earch **F**or **E**xtraterrestrial **I**ntelligence.

3. SETI scientists study stars in our galaxy to find out which ones may be hosts to extraterrestrial intelligence. They use receivers and try to "listen in" on radio signals that ETs may be sending.

Receiving Signals

1. Ask students to imagine they are SETI scientists, pointing a radio telescope at a star cluster. As they hear messages, they vote thumbs up if they think it may be a message from ETs, thumbs down if not, to the side if not sure.

2. Imitate the sound of static, or play the first sound on the tape.

3. Note their votes, and let them discuss the reasons. Scientists call a signal like this "noise." It is produced naturally by some objects in space, and is not a sign of intelligent life.

4. Announce the signal from a second star cluster. Repeat the sound of static. You should expect students to give a thumbs-down.

5. Tell students to imagine the radio telescope pointed at a different star cluster, picking up more radio waves. Make steady beeps at regular intervals or play the third sound. Have them vote.

Get Connected!

Get the *GEMS Network News*

our free educational newsletter filled with—

Updates on GEMS activities and publications.
Suggestions from GEMS enthusiasts around the country.
Strategies to help you and your students succeed.
Information about workshops and leadership training.
Announcements of new publications and resources.

Be part of a growing national network of people who are committed to activity-based science and math education. Stay connected with the GEMS Network News. If you don't already receive the Network News, simply return the attached postage-paid card.

For more information about GEMS call (510) 642-7771, or write to GEMS, Lawrence Hall of Science, University of California, Berkeley, California 94720-5200.

GEMS activities are easy-to-use and effective. They engage students in cooperative, hands-on science and math explorations, while introducing key principles and concepts.

More than 60 GEMS Teacher's Guides and Handbooks have been developed at the Lawrence Hall of Science–the Public science center at the University of California Berkeley–and tested in thousands of classrooms nationwide. There are many more to come–along with local GEMS workshops and GEMS centers and Network Sites springing up across the nation to provide support, training, and resources for you and your colleagues!

Get Connected!
www.lhs.berkeley.edu/GEMS

Yes!

Sign me up for a free subscription to the

GEMS Network News

filled with ideas, information, and strategies that lead to Great Explorations in Math and Science!

Name_____

Address_____

City_____ State_____ Zip_____

How did you find out about GEMS? (Check all that apply.)
❏ word of mouth ❏ conference ❏ ad ❏ workshop ❏ other: _____

❏ In addition to the *GEMS Network News,* please send me a free catalog of GEMS materials.

GEMS
Lawrence Hall of Science
University of California
Berkeley, California 94720-5200
(510) 642-7771

Ideas◄

Suggestions◄

Resources◄

Sign up now for a free subscription to the *GEMS* Network News!

that lead to Great Explorations
in Math and Science!

LHS GEMS

LH68
101 Lawrence Hall of Science # 5200

Get Connected!
www.lhs.berkeley.edu/GFMS

6. Tell students this actually happened in 1967. Scientists even called the sources of the signals LGMs, for "little green men!" They later learned such signals are from collapsed stars called *pulsars*, not signs of life.

7. Tell students to imagine that we've picked up more radio waves from another star cluster. Make an irregular pattern of beeps or play the fourth sound. Have students vote.

8. A complex repeating signal sounds as if it must have been made by someone on purpose. Repeating patterns such as this are exactly what SETI scientists are searching for, but they have not received them…yet.

What Kind Of Message?

1. Ask what kind of languages ETs might use. Explain that human languages are spoken or visual, and can be recorded in many ways. Extraterrestrial languages could be similar or completely different.

2. Briefly brainstorm methods of communication used by humans and other animals. How might extraterrestrial lifeforms communicate with each other?

3. It is thought that ETs able to send messages would have at least one thing in common with us—the ability to send and receive radio signals. Radio signals are the only practical way we know to send a message huge distances across space.

4. Ask students if they can think of any way to make messages understood by anyone—no matter what language—that could be sent by radio waves.

5. SETI scientists sent a message using a mathematically-coded picture, assuming that a culture intelligent enough to build radio receivers is likely to recognize the mathematical patterns and decode the picture.

6. The simplest code for sending a picture by radio signals is a "binary code." It has only two types of signals. A bar code on an item from a store is a binary code in which the two signals are "black" and "white."

7. Binary codes are a way to store and communicate information. Computers work entirely in binary codes, as do digital TVs.

Decoding a Practice Message

1. One way to make a picture in binary code is by using a rectangular grid of small squares. Each small square piece of the picture is called a **bit** and each bit is either black or white.

2. Pass out A Binary Message. Tell students you have a set of 80 bits, a binary code, for them to turn into a picture.

3. The grid must be a rectangle with 80 squares. Is there more than one way? Have them come up with a few. Students choose grids and outline them on graph paper. (Make sure a grid 16 squares across is chosen, correct for decoding this message—but **don't tell them this.**)

4. Students fill in squares from left to right, completing rows from top to bottom. A "beep" signal means to color in the square, and a "click" signal means to leave the square blank and go on to the next.

5. Instruct students not to distract their classmates. Start reading the list of bits in the signal.

6. After all bits have been read and grids completed, have them look at each other's grids.

7. Remind students this is a message from Earthlings to Earthlings. If ETs sent a picture of one of their written words we would not know their language or way of writing it down.

8. Have students recall the signals that seemed to be from intelligent ETs. Tell them to imagine those signals have been decoded into pictures—in the next session they will get to figure out what the message might mean.

Session 2: Interpreting a Message From Space

Getting Ready

Copy the seven pages of the Message from Space for each group, plus copy to post, and a transparency. Also make transparency of Grid for Message. Set up overhead projector. Place transparencies nearby.

Making Contact

1. Remind students the messages have been decoded from a binary signal, allegedly received by a radio telescope from a distant star cluster.

2. Students work to figure out the message. Pass out the first page. Give groups a few minutes of discussion time.

3. Display first page on overhead. Lay Grid for Message on top of it. Then remove the grid. Ask them to share their interpretations.

4. Continue same process with each page. You may want to hand out and discuss pages 5 and 6 together.

5. Point out unexplained portions, and challenge students to continue. The message will be posted so they can write further ideas on post-its.

6. If a message were actually received, there would be no way to know if a particular interpretation was correct or not. The same is true of this simulated message—they will never be told the exact intended meaning.

7. Encourage students to be alert to the news, because a message like this one might someday be received!

Activity 2: Somewhere in the Milky Way— Star Types and Lifezones

Getting Ready

1. Plan your teams based on how many radiometers you can obtain.

2. Prepare the overheads. On the Star Cluster the Message Came From use a permanent marker to lightly color in the stars yellow, red, or blue.

3. Prepare light bulbs.

4. Prepare workspaces by screwing light bulbs into the sockets. Place the in four locations with a full meter of workspace on one side of the bulb.

5. Make the Star Types chart.

Where Did the Message Come From?

1. Invite students on a simulated stargazing session to search for the message's source. Show A Spiral Galaxy and have them describe shapes and structures.

2. We live in a galaxy much like the one shown—the Milky Way. Why can we not see our galaxy in a photograph like this one? [We see the Milky Way from the inside, so the stars are all around us.] Every star we can see is part of the Milky Way Galaxy.

3. Show Many Galaxies. Beyond the Milky Way there are billions of other galaxies. It would take a radio signal over two million years to reach the next nearest major galaxy.

4. Show Star Cluster the Message Came From. In our galaxy there are 400–500 billion stars. If a spaceship could explore one star every minute, it would take nearly a million years to explore every star! **The distances involved are immense! That is why scientists explore the possibility of sending signals—not making visits, or of ETs visiting us.** Stop for any questions students may have.

Lifezones

1. The overhead contains the cluster of stars from which the message allegedly came. What differences do students notice among the stars? If they do not mention color, point it out.

2. Temperature determines star color. There are seven types: blue, blue white, white, yellow white, yellow, orange, and red. Ask about the Sun, then say it is a yellow star. The hottest stars are the bluest; the least hot are the reddest.

3. Students will study each type of star to see which kind of star is most likely to be the kind from which the message could come.

4. No one knows what life elsewhere would be like. We will look for places that could support Earthlike life.

5. What kinds of things does a planet need to support life? (Make sure that water is on the list.) Earth has water in the form of ice, vapor, and clouds, but it is the liquid form that makes life—as we know it—possible.

6. Students will research zones around stars where liquid water may exist. The area where liquid water can exist is referred to as the *lifezone.*

7. Show Our Solar System. Ask where they think there might be liquid water. Scientists believe that Venus, Earth, and Mars all had liquid water at one time, but Earth is the only one at present.

8. The surface of Venus is too hot for liquid water although there are clouds and water vapor high in its atmosphere. The surface of Mars is too cold for anything but ice, but there seem to be dry riverbeds and evidence of flooding long ago. The lifezone of our Sun is the region between Venus and Mars, where it is not too hot, and not too cold.

9. Turn on the light bulbs and explain they represent stars. Tell students they'll visit all the types of stars to take measurements that will show them where the lifezones of these stars are.

Lifezone Measurement (for classes using radiometers)

1. Show students a radiometer and explain they will use them to make the measurements of lifezones.

2. Sometimes they will have to stop the vanes from turning. Show them how by tipping the radiometer slightly.

3. Pass out the Star Types and Lifezones data sheet. Go over the instructions for finding the outer edge and the inner edge of the lifezones. Students will go through the same procedure for each light bulb.

4. Draw attention to the clock to time the rotation.

5. Show students how the meter sticks are taped by each light bulb, and aligned to measure from base of the bulb holder to base of radiometer.

6. Post Star Types chart. Students add data, to the nearest centimeter.

7. Go over safety rules.

8. If there are radiometers for all teams, pass them out and begin. If you for only half, go over the Feeling the Heat section. Have half of the teams do each of the investigations and then switch.

Feeling the Heat (NOT using radiometers)

1. Students will investigate the energy from the light bulbs by seeing how it heats up their hands. Pass out Feeling The Heat sheets.

2. At no time should students touch any of the light bulbs.

3. Demonstrate how to hold hand, palm turned away, and slowly move it toward star, stopping at the slightest amount of warmth.

4. Have students record the distance of their hand from the star in centimeters. Each team member should do this a few times.

5. Suggest that they try it with their eyes closed, with a safety monitor.

6. Students perform same test on each of the four star types.

7. If substituting this for radiometers, tell students this measurement shows how far the lifezone extends (the outer edge of the lifezone). Have them write the team average on the Star Types chart.

Discussion of Results

1. Gently move the four bulbs to the front of the classroom.

2. Draw the students' attention to the results. The area between where it's not too hot and not too cold for liquid water is the lifezone.

3. Do a quick estimated average of each "too hot" and "too cold" result.

4. Plot averages on the line next to the drawing of the star. Draw a line between the two points to indicate the lifezone for that type of star.

5. Draw a few dots to represent planets in and out of each stars' lifezone, Those within may have liquid water and be more likely to evolve life.

6. Ask which stars have the largest and smallest lifezones. The larger the lifezone, the greater chance for a stable planet that could support life.

Star Lifespan Simulation

1. To determine which type of star would be most likely to have a planet that could evolve intelligent life, both lifezone and *lifespan* are important.

2. Scientists think it took over 4 billion years for intelligent life to evolve on Earth. If a star has suitable planets within a lifezone but dies too soon, then intelligent life might not have a chance to evolve.

3. Ask students to imagine each second is a million years. Tell them that you will unplug each star as its time comes up.

4. Choose a clock or watch. Have class say "start" at agreed position. Turn on all light bulbs and announce four new stars have been born.

5. Announce and write the actual times of "death" (the lifespan) on the Star Types chart as you turn out each light.

6. Be quick with the blue star.

7. After the blue and white stars have both "died," tell students to predict when remaining stars will "die," or adjust any predictions.

8. Our Sun is a yellow star. If students not in room at time of "death" of yellow star, it will be on the chart so they can compare predictions.

9. If students will still be in class when yellow star dies, make a note of the time when you will have to pull the plug on it. If not, simply turn out the lights and write the lifespan of the yellow star on the chart.

10. Make sure the red star is shining when students return the next day. At about same time red star was born the day before, or a little later, turn it out, and enter its lifespan on the chart.

Activity 3: Our Neighborhood in the Milky Way—The Solar System

Getting Ready

1. Have the transparency of Our Solar System ready.

2. Fill the containers with 1" to 1 1/2" of water.

What We Know

1. Tell students the class will shift to our solar system. Learning more about it may also help us further interpret the message.

2. Show students Our Solar System and/or a poster. Have them share with a partner then the class what they know about the solar system.

3. Scientists estimate it took about 100 million years for the solar system to form. No one knows how, but scientists have some theories.

4. Challenge students to come up with their own explanations.

Session 1: From a Swirling Cloud

1. Students will use water and pepper as a model for formation of the solar system.

2. Pass out containers of water and stir sticks. Put two shakes of pepper into each container—a scattering of "gas and dust" into "empty space."

3. Gravity pulls the gas and dust together into a swirling mass. Have a student in each team give three or four quick stirs.

4. Have students discuss what they see, then call on students to describe how the system of water and pepper evolves.

5. Ask students how this might represent the formation of the planets. If not mentioned, explain that the clump in the center represents the Sun, and the pieces orbiting it the planets.

6. Give students a few minutes to form, un-form and re-form their solar systems several times, and report new observations.

Session 2: The Solar System—Travel Brochures

Getting Ready

1. Make one copy of Solar System Stations Sign-Up, copies of the Solar System Tour Station, one copy of the Solar System Travel Brochure for each student, and several copies of the fact sheets.

2. Have the craft material together in an easily accessible location.

Introducing the Tour

1. Ask students if they think it would be "cool" to take a tour of the solar system. Have they heard of planetary explorations? [Every planet but Pluto has been investigated by spacecraft with cameras, but no humans. The Moon is the only extraterrestrial site explored by astronauts.]

2. Students will tour the solar system, creating the tour themselves.

3. They should focus on what it would be like to be in their assigned part of the solar system. Is their planet (or other object) in the Sun's lifezone? What would a lifeform encounter there? What would humans need?

4. Challenge each team to put energy into making the stations interesting, so the tour will be enjoyable for the whole class.

5. Distribute Solar System Tour Station sheet and make assignments. When you come to model making, explain that they will get a fact sheet that has the proper diameter. Review **diameter** if necessary.

Describing the Travel Brochure Assignment

1. Each student is responsible for writing a travel brochure. Pass out the Solar System Travel Brochure sheet.

2. As an example of how to include accurate facts in a humorous manner, read the two examples about the Atacama desert aloud.

3. If you've collected some, show students travel brochures.

4. Encourage use of poems, illustrations, models, and comparisons. It can be playful, but factual information should be accurate.

5. Draw station layout on the board.

6. Show students where the garbage bags and craft materials are located.

7. Assign teams to their planetary stations.

8. After teams have selected an astronomical body to work on, distribute fact sheet to the team—one for each student. Brainstorm other resources.

Session 3: Touring the Solar System

Getting Ready

1. Plan where each team will set up its station.

2. Make double-sided copy of Tour of the Solar System for each student.

Preparing the Tour

1. Remind students the message seemed to depict planets in that star system. They can study the planets in our own solar system as a model.

2. Review main things that make a planet suitable for life: proper temperature, liquid water, star with long lifespan.

3. Have your students set up their stations at designated locations, starting with the Sun, then position others in order around the classroom.

4. Distribute Tour of the Solar System sheets. Read aloud questions, to be answered after completing the tour.

5. Show students Chart of Key Life Factors. They should record information about the planets on this chart during the tour.

Beginning the Tour

1. Have teams at their stations. Tell them which direction to move on to the next station at your signal. Allow at least two minutes per station.

2. When all the groups have finished and returned to their original stations, they should respond to the questions.

3. Discuss responses, or discuss: "Using the information you've gathered, where in our solar system besides Earth do you think there might be life?"

Session 4: Putting the Planets in Their Places

Getting Ready

1. Determine locations you will use for the planets in the scale model. The Sun will be in your classroom.

2. For the nearer planets, estimate or pace out the distance from your classroom, and locate some landmark.

3. For the more distant planets and other objects, use a local map.

4. List all the planet and other locations on the chart so that you will be able to locate them with your students in the schoolyard and on the map.

Distances in Space

1. Have students at the station they created. Draw their attention to the size-model of the Sun—in this model the Sun is 1 meter in diameter.

2. Tell each team to hold up their model, and notice the size of the planets relative to the Sun at this scale. Point out some of the large and small planets, and how much smaller they are than the Sun.

3. Ask members of the Earth team to walk around the room, and hold their model against other objects. The Earth seems huge to us—but it appears very small when compared to some of the other objects.

4. In a scale model all objects are reduced by the same proportion. Not only the **sizes** of the objects should be to scale, but the **distances between** the objects should also be to scale.

5. Hold the Earth next to Mercury and ask the class to compare their diameters. Tell students to keep this idea of the scale of Earth's diameter in mind as they consider the distances between the planets.

6. Where in the room might Mercury belong? It will be outside of the room entirely! Direct the Mercury team to the location you've designated.

7. Ask students to imagine how many Earths it would span the distance from the Sun to Mercury. [About 4,500 Earths lined up side by side]

8. Using Earth-diameters is one way to compare sizes, but it is awkward for extremely large distances. Astronomers use the average distance from the Sun to the Earth as a standard measure, or Astronomical Unit (AU).

9. Direct the Venus team to its designated location, then the Earth team. Continue with the Moon, then Mars, if space allows.

10. The main ingredient of the solar system is empty space.

11. Ask the Asteroid Belt team how practical they think it would be to take their asteroid model to its typical place, 300 meters (about a quarter of a mile) away. Ask the same question of the Saturn team.

Plotting on a Map

1. Use the local map to mark the locations of all the planets and other space objects that are too distant to fit in your schoolyard

2. Remind students that the planets are not fixed in one location in space, but orbit around the Sun at that distance from the Sun.

3. Ask where the nearest star system, Alpha Centauri, would be located in this model. It would be about 3/4 the distance around the globe..

4. Spaceships can travel at about 25,000 mph. At that speed, it would take about 120,000 years to get to Alpha Centauri, the *closest* star system. This is the main reason SETI scientists believe it unlikely ETs could come to Earth—the distances are enormous!!

Activity 4: Dear Extraterrestrials...

Getting Ready

1. Have on hand the transparencies of the message from space, and of the Arecibo, Pioneer, and Voyager messages.

2. Have a piece of paper to keep the key to the Arecibo message covered until after students interpret it for themselves.

Reviewing the Message from Space

1. Students are going to design a message to send back to the ETs who sent the message. Ask what information would be important to send.

2. Review message and find out what further ideas students have. What information seems to have been important to those who sent it?

3. To communicate information about "how big" or "how many" would seem to require mathematics. Examine the message to see if those who sent it tried to communicate a measuring or numbering system.

Looking at Examples

1. Show students Arecibo message. Keep the explanation covered. It was designed by a SETI scientist, Frank Drake, and broadcast into space as a binary signal.

2. Challenge students to interpret the Arecibo message.

3. Gradually uncover the key to the Arecibo message and explain each section. Ask for comments. Ask, "How might distant lifeforms interpret the picture of a person and the radio telescope if they didn't know what the real ones look like?"

4. Show students plaque attached to Pioneer space probes. This was not a binary-coded message, but a picture attached to a pair of space probes that have now left the solar system. Perhaps millions of years from now, some ETs may find it!

5. Encourage a short discussion. Ask students if they would have shown people with or without clothes. If wearing clothes, what kind of clothes?

6. Show students Voyager transparency. On these space probes was a "Sounds of Earth" recording, with a picture showing a device to play it. What sounds would students choose? Show them list that was included.

Making the Message

1. Pass out two pieces of paper and drawing materials. Other members of the class will interpret their messages, so they should be secretive.

2. Have students list what they want to include. A message with much information may be interesting, but a simple one easier to understand.

3. Have students draw their picture-message twice. One drawing should be with the list of things they are trying to communicate. On the other, just the drawing. This shows the message the "ETs" would actually see.

4. Students could turn their pictures into binary messages on graph paper.

5. Have teams exchange and interpret the messages.

6. Reconvene class. Have a team show message they "received" and explain interpretation. Continue discussing messages as time allows.

Activity 5: Making a Planetary System

Getting Ready

1. Copy the Red Stars sheet onto red paper, Yellow Stars onto yellow, White Stars onto white, and Blue Stars onto blue. Cut them out roughly, into squares. Put each set into an envelope labeled with the star's color.

2. Make one copy of Strip Compass for each team and cut it out. Also make one copy of The Distant Planetary System sheet for each team.

3. Add measurements for rocky planet zones and gas giant zones.

Introducing the Activity

1. Now that students have studied the solar system they will try to learn more about the system whose inhabitants sent the message from space.

2. We only have our solar system to work from, but can assume many of the rules apply in other planetary systems. At the same time, we can also assume that a huge number of variations can occur!

3. They will be using the planetary system they design as a setting for a science fiction story.

4. Show transparency of final page of message. Point out the section at the top—it appears to be our solar system, with its nine planets.

5. Point out section at bottom—it appears to be the ETs' planetary system. It appeared to have six planets, and the message seemed to show that the fourth planet underwent some kind of drastic change.

Making the Planetary Systems Suitable for Life

1. Tell students the only information they have about the planetary system is what they can learn from the message and what they have learned from studying stars and planetary systems.

2. Tell students the message does not appear to indicate what type of star the system has. They will use information about lifezones and lifespans to choose type of star at the center. Information has been added to chart about where rocky and gas giant planets are found.

3. Review criteria students used to search for possible life locations when they took the tour: rocky surface; liquid water; enough gravity to hold an atmosphere and liquid water; survivable atmosphere; a source of energy.

4. Point out that a planetary system suitable for life would also need to have no major interference from comets or asteroids, and a planetary orbit that would not cause too much fluctuation in temperature.

5. Show students the colored papers to use as the stars at the centers of their systems and ask them to trim them into circles.

6. Encourage students to be creative, yet realistic. They should keep in mind where life might evolve. Encourage creative variations.

Making and Using Strip Compasses

1. You may use tape measures or rulers, but strip compass allows students to mark off the zones and draw orbits. If you do not already have strip compasses, show how to make and use them.

2. Demonstrate how to measure and mark how far the lifezones would extend. Demonstrate the rocky planet and gas giant lifezones.

3. For each planet they draw an arc centered on the star for the orbit, and draw the planet. The sizes should indicate relative sizes of planets. Point out that this model will not be to scale.

Designing Planetary Systems

1. Pass out the strip compasses, pencils, and sheets of paper.

2. When students finish designing, distribute Planetary System sheet.

3. Tell students they have just created a model using data available to them. Model making is a major part of the science of astronomy.

4. Encourage students to keep up with the news, and compare their models with newly-discovered planetary systems.

Critical Reading Assignment

Which articles are based on scientific thinking, and which are sensationalized fictions?

Activity 6: Science Fiction Stories

Getting Ready

1. Decide whether you want students to work independently or
in teams. Duplicate one copy of Science Fiction Ideas per student or team.

2. Place the student models of planetary systems so all can examine them while working on their stories.

Talking about Science Fiction

1. Ask students to share brief comments about **science fiction** books, movies, or TV shows. They will write science fiction stories.

2. Remind students the planetary systems they designed will serve as the settings for their stories.

3. Their stories may be as strange, but that they should try to show how such things could actually happen.

Planning the Stories

1. Many great stories have only a few main characters, and told from one perspective. Remind them of the story line hinted at in the message.

2. Students can tell what happened to the planet, why distant lifeforms sent the message, what happened when Earth replied, or about the everyday life of an extraterrestrial.

3. Ask students to imagine that they are on a planet that supports life in the planetary system they designed.

4. Go through the questions on the Science Fiction Ideas sheet, distribute it, then have students fill out the sheet and create their stories.